Lesser Lives

NITIN SINHA is Senior Research Fellow at Leibniz-Zentrum Moderner Orient (ZMO), Berlin. He was the principal investigator of a three-year project (2015–18) entitled, 'Domestic Servants in Colonial South Asia', funded by the European Research Council (ERC). A regular contributor to the *Wire* and various journals, he has written *Communication and Colonialism in Eastern India: Bihar, 1760s–1880s* and co-edited two volumes of *Servants' Pasts* on the history of domestic servants in India. He has taught at the universities of Humboldt and York, among other institutions. He recently won the prestigious ERC Consolidator Grant for his project on a social history of time in South Asia.

PRABHAT KUMAR is Assistant Professor at the Centre for the Study of Developing Societies, New Delhi. He has taught history at the Presidency University, Kolkata. His areas of research include the literary, visual and cultural histories of north India. He is presently a fellow at the M. S. Merian–R. Tagore International Centre for Advanced Studies: Metamorphosis of the Political (ICAS:MP), Delhi.

Advance Praise for *Lesser Lives*

'While reading this book, the reader will definitely scrutinize their home. A home is not just a home; it is also a workplace – not for those who live in it but for those whose regularized entrance at different times maintains its smooth running. A document of our homes ... [*Lesser Lives*] promises to open up the closed windows of our prejudices. Nitin Sinha and Prabhat Kumar have transformed the everyday and mundane details of the household into an epical form by bringing invisible characters to light. This is an exemplary piece of work which will become a landmark in opening new debates on contemporary social issues. A book like this should be made available in every language'

– **Ravish Kumar**, journalist and author of *The Free Voice*

'Literature holds up a mirror to society and presents us with images from social realities that we often tend to ignore. A wonderful selection of stories from the beginning of the twentieth century until the 1960s–70s, [*Lesser Lives*] takes us into a world which is normally kept hidden from us: the world of the domestic help who are usually infantilized, denied personhood or equal treatment. These stories give a voice to the desires, longings and emotions of a marginalized section of the society ... The servant becomes the central figure of these stories in various social settings, ranging from rural to urban, zamindari to middle-class and Hindu and Muslim households and we see the complex realities of their lives as real persons, not just an invisible piece of furniture, meant to make our lives easier'

– **Rana Safvi**, author of *City of My Heart* and *The Forgotten Cities of Delhi*

Lesser Lives

Stories of Domestic Servants in India

Edited by
NITIN SINHA
PRABHAT KUMAR

Translated by
PRABHAT KUMAR

PAN

First published 2021 by Pan
an imprint of Pan Macmillan Publishing India Private Limited
707, Kailash Building,
26, K. G. Marg, New Delhi – 110 001
www.panmacmillan.co.in

Pan Macmillan, 6 Briset St, Farringdon, London EC1M 5NR
Associated companies throughout the world
www.panmacmillan.com

ISBN 978-93-89109-74-0

1 3 5 7 9 8 6 4 2

Typeset in Aldine401 BT by R. Ajith Kumar, New Delhi
Printed and bound in India by
Replika Press Pvt. Ltd.

Contents

Introduction

A Second Look at Our Households

NITIN SINHA AND PRABHAT KUMAR

The everyday life of the Indian middle class has significantly changed in the last thirty to forty years. Modern techniques and technologies have brought new ideas about society and family: there's comfort from air conditioners and coolers in the bedroom, the pleasure of savouring iced drinks due to refrigerators, the ease of washing clothes in the washing machine and the option of warming up food in the microwave. A large number of women now go out of the home to work and to earn a living. The structure of the family and household has also gradually changed. Joint families are fast disappearing and nuclear families, particularly in urban centres, as a result of migration due to marriage, for employment, or both, are becoming the norm.

But then, as the saying goes, the more things change, the more they remain the same. Domestic servants in various avatars – domestic aid, domestic help, domestic staff – are still permanent features of Indian middle-class households.

They were present in the days when cooking was done on the *goytha* or *lakdi chulha* (earthen oven that uses cow dung or firewood for fuel); they are present when induction plates adorn the beautiful modular kitchens. They were present in the past; they continue to be indispensable in the present. Of course, the nature of the service, the ways of hiring, the gender component of the service class and the aspirations of the servants themselves have all changed. But the reality of their quintessential presence is unchanged. It peeps through, perhaps not so surprisingly, in moments of repugnant realities. In 2016, when a distasteful advert on the website Bookmybai.com encouraged the man to forget about diamonds and, instead, gift the wife a maid, the reality of 'new India' and its crumbling domesticity was revealed. The cracks due to the burden of housework, which disproportionately falls on the woman, needed to be cemented not by conjugal sharing of work but by hiring a maid. The starkness of unequal engagement with domestic maids becomes visible when extreme incidents of apathy come to the fore. In 2018, a picture taken inside a Delhi metro train went viral on social media, in which a maid was sitting on the floor while her employer and the child were on the seat. Servants are expected to conform to a specific set of manners and gestures and adhere to a specific way of talking that displays subordination. The lavish display of technology from the bedroom to the kitchen and from the bathroom to the stairs of the apartments in high-rise 'societies' has failed to make paid human labour in household chores redundant. In the eighteenth century, there were different servants for different tasks. For instance, an *aabdar* cooled the water with the use of saltpetre and a *farash* swung the fly whisk standing behind his reclining master and mistress. Who knows, in some glass-sealed apartments with rooftop gardens, there are special washing machine operators and dedicated carpet cleaners.

The paid labour in these households tends to remain invisible, but that is our misplaced way of thinking. First, we must realize and accept that the long history of institutional nexus between law, method of employment, mechanisms of policing and the power wielded by the employing classes have rendered domestic servants invisible. Second, their (enforced) invisibility sits ironically with their quintessential presence and demand in well-to-do households that depend on their labour. Even in households of average means, a part-time maid would come to clean the dishes and the house. And third, their invisibility is also a product of the expected norms of performing and maintaining social and class differences between the employers and the employees. Such boundaries are not only to be observed within households but, as the metro image showed, also outside. The 'invisibilization' is a product of this boundary-making exercise which is routinely observed and breached. By sitting silently on the floor of the metro rail, the domestic maid observes the boundary as well as makes herself visible to the public gaze.

The inevitable dependence of middle-class households on paid domestic labour often reveals itself in moments of crises. It has come to the fore most recently during the series of Covid-19 lockdowns. For any period in history, an 'episode' or an 'event' that disrupts normalcy is perhaps the best gauge to understand the nature of that normalcy itself. The crisis reveals the comfort of certainty. This is true for our times as well. As in the routinized normal times, these servants, aides and helps remain invisible, the disruption in the routine exposes their presence and reveals our dependence on them.

If we turn our gaze to the most vibrant 'archive' of our contemporary life – the WhatsApp group forwards and memes – it is hard to miss how 'humour' is deployed to gloss over the troubled domesticity of these households. In one joke widely shared on such groups, the coronavirus is said to have brought about significant change in the majority of men's lives: instead of bar and Scotch, Vim bar, a popular dish-washing soap, and Scotchbrite, an equally popular brand of dish scrubs, have been placed in their hands. Indian men finally claimed to do domestic work, albeit grudgingly! In another, a woman endearingly tells her husband she would not allow him to go back to work after the lockdown is over. On being asked for the reason, she says that she likes his way of doing household chores more than the maid's. Amidst the slew of laughing and 'ROFL' smileys that these jokes evoke in virtual spaces of bonding, little noticed is the fact that humour has effectively created a myth that in Indian households domestic work is shared equally between men and women, suggesting that in the post-coronavirus world, employing domestic maids will become a thing of the past. Ironically, the reality was captured in the unpleasant advert that came out in 2016: maids will remain the inevitable provider of labour and care in the households of their employers; in fact, in a rather objectified manner of being more valuable than a piece of diamond jewellery.

In the past, globally, it was imagined that the system of paid domestic work would come to an end. In the West, by the mid-twentieth century, the presence of paid domestic workers declined to a great extent. In India, around the same period, employing a domestic servant was explained through the incidences of poverty, illiteracy and the caste system. It was nevertheless thought that as these social and economic evils would disappear with time, so would the widespread practice of keeping domestic servants. As humankind was imagined to move towards progress and modernity, the 'feudal' piquancy attached to the system of paid domestic work was believed to become a relic of the past. The reality turned out to be otherwise, both worldwide and definitely in India.

From Mexican nannies in North America, Filipino maids in the Middle East and eastern European cleaners in rich western European countries, there has indeed been a resurgence of paid domestic work, which in turn has produced many forms of inequalities. Some commentators even call it 'neo-slavery'; others point to the hidden network of trafficking, particularly of young girls in this business of providing servants or service providers to households. In India, too, when the demand for regularizing domestic work was made in the last two decades (by bringing workers under the protective umbrella of legal and social security laws), many cases of girls being trafficked into big cities from poorer regions such as Bihar, Odisha, Jharkhand, Chhattisgarh and West Bengal were brought to light. According to Global March Against Child Labour, out of around 215 million child labourers globally, more than fifteen million are in domestic service, a majority of them young girls.

For instance, in one of the many cases of this type, Ratni, a fourteen-year-old girl from Jharkhand, was brought to New Delhi as a domestic worker. She was about to be sold as a slave into prostitution when she was rescued by the Bachpan Bachao Andolan.[1] The role of lawyers and activists has been noteworthy in taking up the cause of regularization of work and service providers or recruiting agencies. According to Jeet Singh, in a policy brief of 2014, the likely market for child labour in the National Capital Region of Delhi can cause a circulation of as much as ₹205 crores to ₹1,554 crores of illegal money in the market. The agencies make huge amounts of money in this system of procuring servants from 'backward' regions and placing them in urban households. The growing number of unions and associations of domestic workers has indeed played a crucial role in the demand for better regulation of work and in securing better working conditions.[2]

Since Independence in 1947, seventeen private bills on this issue have been moved by different parliamentarians across party lines in both houses of the parliament. From the initial focus on regulating working conditions, the last few (introduced as recently as 2017) have expanded the scope of the definition of both work and worker. While the vocabulary of the employer class has inched away from 'servants' to 'helps', the legislative demand is for recognizing them as proper 'workers'. The paid domestic's work at the household, goes the argument, should be seen in the same way as work performed at a site of construction or in a factory. And this is the crux of the contention – the labouring rights of the domestic servants/workers would be very difficult to achieve unless they are seen as workers. This would, however, mean that the household of the employer needs to be recognized as a 'worksite' – a place of employment – to be governed by certain well-defined laws and regulations. But our sense of the division between the public and the private spheres of life comes in between this way of thinking. There is a palpable discomfort in letting law define the household, little realizing that perhaps there is no aspect of life untouched by the shadow of law. Yet, the inviolable sanctity of the home as a private set of relationships that includes domestics reigns large in our imagination.

The languages and bonds of kinship ties – fictional and established – expressed through terms such as 'kaka' and 'kaki', used for elderly servants, draw them into the world of private, emotional ties with their employers. The presence of the state or the law is then resisted to govern this relationship. Yet, emotional affinity is only one half of the story, that too, most likely a tenuous one. In many cases, as seen in films and noticed in literature, employers are also not averse to invoking the authority of the state when they wish to do so. The common refrain to the servant – 'will report you to the police' – allows the employers, primarily due to their class position, to discipline or scare their servants using the authority of the police. The fictive or imagined kinship ties break down in that moment. This is noticeable in many of the stories in this volume. For instance, the story 'Bahadur' beautifully captures the waning bond (son-like) established with the newly arrived boy-servant. Soon, beatings, reprimands and suspicion of theft replace the language of affection, barring the reality of the difference between 'son' and 'son-like'. In 'Ratnaprabha', the woman protagonist of the same name first gets the street lad, who later becomes her servant, thrashed by her driver. On noticing that this beating has led to no 'reform' in him, she then threatens to get him beaten up by the police.

Bridget Anderson, a scholar who has written on the subject of domestic servants, had a fascinating encounter while interviewing a servant. The latter told Anderson that the problem is not that the employer might treat her as a slave, the problem is in *treating* her like family. Many researchers have pointed out the constrictions and the manipulative possibilities that emerge out of this claim and the imposition of fictive familial bonds. Servants also indeed use this language of bond to claim and demand more help, usually monetary, from their employers. But the argument about bracketing emotions into the logic of law is a misleading one. Law and regulation are being wielded to better regulate working conditions. They are being demanded to place accountability and transparency in the system of hiring and employment, and in the treatment of domestic workers at their workplaces in either one household where they are live-ins or in multiple houses where they work part-time. None of this should actually affect the emotional connect between employers and employees. Currently, the absence of well-defined parameters of work (leave, absence, pension, etc.) together with the privilege of class which allows access to state power weighing heavily in favour of employers makes this relationship structurally unequal. After all, following the controversy at Mahagun Moderne Society in Noida, it was the *basti*s of servants that were demolished and not the apartments where the employers resided.

In the last two decades, various studies have shown why legal regulation of domestic work is important to improve the working conditions of domestic workers. It relates to establishing a transparent and accountable system of hiring, limiting the hours of work and leave, having provisions for redressal of grievances and abuse and covering them under pension schemes and other social security benefits. This has been globally acknowledged, with the International Labour Organization (ILO) Domestic Workers Convention, 2011, (no. 189) stressing the need to provide 'decent working conditions' for domestic servants. India signed the convention in 2011 but has not ratified it so far.

Seen from the employers' side, there would be many who would genuinely question the legal 'intervention' in the organization of their household work. They would insist that domestic work is a different kind of work that cannot be treated like work performed in a factory. Further, they would claim they are always or often benevolent to their servants. They would allege that the problem arises because of the fault of the servants: they commit theft, they are disloyal, irregular, lazy, slow, insolent and so on. 'Whatever good you do to them, they won't change their conduct' is the common refrain from the employers' side.

Harbouring a benevolent attitude towards servants might definitely be true for some employers, but benevolence cannot be the basis of policy formulation. The benevolence, with time, can start thinning, as it happens with the protagonist of the story 'Wo Chor Tha'. Lakshmi Babu shows extreme dependence and trust in Laloo, his personal attendant. But when the theft of his personal effects and money begins, Lakshmi Babu turns distant. He starts doubting Laloo even if he does not blame him directly. Laloo also feels the growing distance but cannot do much to undo the changed relationship. The relationships formed on the basis of loyalty and benevolence, therefore, can turn very tenuous. In a work relationship based on a waged form of service exchange, the question is: why should the conditions of work remain completely undefined and left to be dealt only with trust, emotion, charity and loyalty?

When a large segment of the population earns its living by doing dishes and cleaning floors in others' homes, the dignity of work and personhood cannot be left at the choice of benevolence practised by others. This is the fundamental difference which needs to be hammered in. Paid domestic work is not seen as 'dignified' work. Benevolence of some employers is not enough to restore the dignity of the human being who performs paid domestic work. This workforce is extremely vast, and we do not even know its exact extent – the number of domestic servants in India ranges anywhere between four and ninety million according to a 2011 report on domestic workers by the ILO. The personalized forms of 'welfare' and 'support' cannot be the bedrock for matters of life and livelihood. Generosity is not a substitute for accountability which, as reasoned by experts, can only be achieved through law. Such a vast workforce, that has not even been concretely enumerated, cannot be left at the mercy of the benevolence of employers.

Further, the historical lineage of this line of thinking – that the household is a place of benevolence for servants – is premised upon a greater degree of infantilization of servants. During the debate on one of the first bills that was introduced in the parliament in 1959, it was said that employers should treat their servants as children which would be beneficial for both sides. A fictive tie of kinship is invoked to establish harmony. This infantilization goes even further back in time – a colonial official in his early twenties would call an Indian servant in the fifties a 'boy'. It would not be wrong to mention that such an epithet is widely used in Indian households in contemporary times as well. Denial of adulthood extends to denial of personhood. It is no surprise that ILO's convention linked the idea of 'decent work' to the universal concept of human dignity. Whether servants are treated with the same kind of dignity as is expected in an exchange between two *equal* human beings is worth reflecting upon.

II

While the struggle for recognizing domestic work as 'work' continues in the political and legal arenas, let us turn to literature to both understand and reflect better on the nature of this relationship. There is a reason why we think literature can tell us something more about the texture of this relationship than what can be gainfully gleaned from court cases or newspaper reports. We read stories and through them rediscover the world around and inside us. Literature is a cultural document that informs us about society as well as reconstitutes social realities. Literature not only communicates but also mediates and shapes social reality. In addition, very crucially, literature documents the social experience of our everyday life. It provides a sensory texture to complex reality and, in doing so, makes it affective and graspable. It empowers us to perceive the beauty and oddity of our mundane and everyday lives otherwise lost in routine encounters and daily recurrences. In simple terms, it makes us sensible and sensitive. We hope that readers will have a similar experience while going through this collection of stories.

The stories presented here are as much about the domestic servant as they are about the master and mistress and their family members. They are, in fact, stories of middle-class families and their domestic lives. These stories bring out the functional and emotional dimensions of interdependent lives. The lives of people like us – the readers of this book. And in doing so, they also bring out the lives of our maids and helps. They come and work in their employers' homes every day and then they retreat to reappear the next day. Ever-present in our homes as they are, they play a crucial role in maintaining and sustaining the tranquil rhythm of domestic lives. The domestic servants visibly manage our lives at home as well as outside in various capacities (as cooks, ayahs, cleaners, sweepers or providers of other services and care work). We develop affective relationships with them. In this exchange, they are loved, feared, trusted, suspected, respected and humiliated. When their routine presence is interrupted, we immediately acknowledge them for their absence. We also acknowledge them when we reflect upon our (domestic) lives, as we can notice in many of the stories in this book, particularly in two of Mahadevi Varma's stories, 'Rama' and 'Sabia'. The reminiscences of childhood and the kindness of character help us see the presence of servants, quite centrally, in the lives of master/mistress-narrators. Sometimes, they come across not as devoted, loyal persons but as defiant ones. The beggar boy on whom Ratnaprabha takes pity, while also simultaneously getting him disciplined through physical beating, does not say much. His silent mode of communication irks and fascinates his mistress. Later, as he becomes her close attendant because she wants it so, we notice the inversion of the relationship. Mangal (as he is given a name) becomes the master, who through his patience, silence and eventual departure provides a closure to his nonchalant, restless mistress who finally ends up seeing herself as his devotee, admirer and, in fact, worshipper.

These stories remind us that literature is also an arena where we can observe to a greater extent the complex totality of the lives of servants. When events of conflict – usually crime – get reported in the media, we only learn about the moment of encounter. In contrast, these stories deal with the quotidian flow of life, emotion, moral boundaries and dilemmas as well as changes in the life cycles of both masters/mistresses and servants. The fictive narratives offer a better grasp of reality. In order to illuminate lesser-known historical subjects, such as domestic servants and their irreducibly complex social milieu, literature becomes indispensable on at least two counts. One, literature is complementary as well as an alternative to official and state-sanctioned narratives. Archives are organized based on what the state requires to preserve. Literature, on the contrary, aims to capture social reality. What seems socially relevant gets recorded in literature. Two, literature provides multilayered narratives of the historical–cultural world we inhabit. Hence, it provides a richer texture of social relationships.

However, just as there are challenges in working with 'archival sources', they also exist in relation to literary sources. After all, literature is bound to contain the element of fiction. It is a mirror of reality, albeit not reality per se. It also contains 'perspective' as much as state documents do. Literature is borne out of literary cultures that change with time. Genres change, sensibilities change, and so do the ways of thinking around social and political issues. Cultures in themselves are never static. Literature allows us to map the changing culture of relationships between masters/mistresses and their servants in the past and how they have mutated into their present forms.

In India, conventionally, the histories of non-literate peoples are difficult to write. Workers, peasants, servants – these groups have usually left no accounts in their own words. Unlike Victorian Britain, we do not find letters and diaries written by servants about their work and life. This is not to say that those who leave historical accounts in their own words necessarily make the task of writing their histories easier. Stories, therefore, become one crucial resource of excavating the lives of unlettered men and women. And yet, difficulty persists. It is evident while reading the story 'Ratnaprabha'. While the story revolves around two characters, Ratnaprabha and the street boy-turned-servant, there is another servant in the story. He is the driver of Ratnaprabha, present in the narrative to simply receive orders from his mistress. When we notice this kind of formulaic presence of lesser lives in stories or other types of documents, we realize the insurmountable difficulty in bringing such characters out of the wooden frame they have has been boxed in.

In toto, these stories present domestic servants in myriad ways. At times, they are present to symbolically refer to the annoying changes of the 'new times'; sometimes they are present to reinscribe the value of an idealized tradition. Premchand's 'Maidservant', which resolves that it is better to do housework on one's own than hire servants, does both at the same time.

Sometimes, the stories use the servant figure as a prop to portray a romantic, melodramatic life journey of success as in 'The Whip of Fortune'; other times, the servants become the bearer of those voices and desires that the society does not want to hear or notice. However, their desires, which baffle, surprise and confuse even them are perhaps too obscene or repugnant to be known socially. 'On the Boil' and 'Blouse' lay bare the inner selves of male adolescent servants. Through their presence, we see an interlinked life of authority and submission, order and defiance, shame and revelation.

What we also notice are the links between the private and the public. Ratnaprabha goes to the riverbank every morning – an open public space – and, in that recourse, brings home a servant literally from the streets. Bahadur, on the other hand, runs away from his home to avoid his mother's beatings and appears as a servant in a distant place. Here also, after the initial love and care, rebuke and beating become part of his everyday experience. Their entry in and exit from the households tell us how, in spite of the guarded sanctity of the home, the paid labour we depend on keeps these households at the cusp of the private and the public. The runaway boy-servant might reappear working in a tea shack on the highway or in a town dhaba as 'Chhotu'. This character is central in the story 'Dajyu'. While taking orders from customers, Madan develops an instant affinity and closeness with Jagdish Babu as they are both from the same region. The initial warmth nevertheless dissipates and Madan has to take back his fond epithet (Dajyu, meaning big brother) for Jagdish Babu. In that course, he brings back for himself the 'public' identity of being called a 'boy'. In the fleeting glimpse of him beyond a waiter-boy – Madan, who has a family elsewhere that he misses – returns to the identity of 'boy', a waiter serving customers their orders.

These stories not only represent the interwoven lives of masters and mistresses and their domestics but also allow a peep into the world of servants beyond the space of their workplace. Rama, Mangar, Bahadur, Dajyu, Sabia, Laloo and Madan – all the servants in the stories have their own families and relationships. While they face hardships in making their livelihoods, they also find joy in their familial ties. These stories allow us to see what a servant's life could possibly look like in totality. While appearing as shadows of their masters and mistresses, the servants' personhoods are visibly recognizable in literary representations. In other words, by being able to read their words as well as silences, we get a sense of not only how they acted but also about how they thought.

As literature is premised upon the use of language, let us raise here a fundamental point on the use of language to describe servants. Our 'liberal' values have recently made us aware that it is impolite to call domestic workers 'servants'. They are 'helps'. We consciously use the words 'us' and 'they' as the English-speaking readership of this book would largely fall under the category of us, that is, the servant-hiring classes. The word servant – the Hindi *naukar* or *naukarani* – perhaps reeks of a 'feudal' past. A sense of stinking rawness of domination emanates from these words, which we want to avoid. With our modern sensibility mixed with a pinch of shame and guilt, and a dose of fairness and politeness, we want to sound respectful in this unequal relationship. The question is: are we really being respectful towards them by changing the term itself – by shifting from Hindi to English along the change of the terms from 'naukar'/'naukarani'/'servant' to 'help'? If the word 'servant' starkly offends by reminding us of unambiguous inequality, then the word 'help' makes the work done by domestics appear benign. One can argue that the term 'help' is a camouflage born out of an urbane sensibility, which fundamentally devalues the work performed by domestics: the 'hidden' meaning or intention is that the master or mistress of the household remains the actual 'doer' of all the chores. The cooks, the maids, the cleaners, the ayahs, they simply help. Is that really the case? The transition should be from the servant to the worker without the intermediate 'aid' of help.

III

In this volume, we have chosen to bring together eleven short stories originally written in Hindi and Urdu by leading practitioners of their craft. This is just a small sample from the large swathe of stories written in various Indian languages, which, of course, need to be read in their original but also deserve to be translated widely. In our effort here, we have focused on the stories that were originally published in Hindi or Urdu, thus offering a glimpse of broadly northern and eastern Indian households, work and relationships that spin around paid work. But while our choice of language may appear limiting to some, within this selection, we have covered a range of households, but more importantly, sketched a narrative in a way that will not be regarded by the young readers of the book as artefacts of an ancient past. They cover the period of the twentieth century and indicate the presence of the immediate past in our times. These stories roughly cover the period from the beginning of the twentieth century until the 1960s–70s. As most of these stories are unavailable in English,[3] they particularly appealed to us for the purpose of translation. The anthology caters to both literary and progressive political projects of our modern times: the aim is to present stories about servants, or to re-read servants into well-known stories, and by doing so, come close to understanding the muted speech and voice of the marginal sections of the society. The stories re-focus the anatomy of home from the shoulders and eyes of its servants; they open the precincts of home, which is narrowly imagined as a closed space of leisure and desire involving husband/man, wife/woman and child–parent. By way of translating these stories into English, the anthology attempts to bring the subject of domestic servants into the domain of wider public readership beyond academia. It aspires to make readers take a second look at their homes.

The various registers of the language and idioms of expression are key to unlocking the routinized presence of lesser lives in the households. Their acute understanding is indispensable for comprehending how the command of authority flows through silences, how the effect of unsaid words sometimes lingers longer than those that are directly uttered. In such a translation project as this one, capturing both words and silences is indeed a challenging task and we hope that we have managed satisfactorily. This, however, also required us to adopt a clear strategy of remaining close and true to the expressions used in the original Hindi. We found it imperative to follow closely the sentence structures not only commonly used in the Hindi language but also in the idiosyncratic forms of expression of these individual storytellers who belong to different genres of writing. We, of course, have made the English text as palatable and smooth as is required for lucid reading, but have deliberately not 'straightened' it to conform to the sensibility of standardized English readership. We have not dropped off any expression that might ring odd to the habituated readers of English prose. The vernacular idiom, expression, edginess and, to an extent, roughness had to be carried over in translation to make the texture of the master-servant relationship evident. In this regard, we have worked more with the burden of a historian's sensibility than with the pleasure of literary scholars or translators.

These stories explore a range of male, female and child-servant characters and their relationships with their employers in a variety of social settings: rural, zamindari, urban, middle-class, Hindu and Muslim households. In most of them, the servant is the central figure of the narrative, often of heroic dimension, which must be read as a literary design rather than necessarily a portrayal of reality. The fact that these litterateurs decided to draw their stories around the figure of the servant and make them heroic deeply points to the existence of an exactly opposite condition. In their quotidian lives, servants usually remain marginal, invisible and unnoticed. In these short stories they have been intentionally made visible.

However, the writers whose stories appear here had their own sensibilities and contexts in mind. They also reflected the concerns of their times. Some located the servants as part of their reminiscences of childhood, as a source of affect, while others located them in the strict and narrow confines of the different chores of the household. Still others used the disprivileged condition of servants to reflect upon the larger politics of class divisions and nationalism. Equally important is that a number of stories bring out the moral–ethical dimension of this relationship. This has been done once again by inversing the 'normal' code of the relationship. Servants have been portrayed to provide the model of rectitude to their masters/mistresses. Servants embody the 'high moral ground' to force readers to reflect how in the normal course of interaction, they are constantly looked down upon with derision and suspicion. However, this usurpation of the high moral ground is also a 'burden' for them – servants retrieve and rescue their employers from their sins and ills by adopting a morally upright position like in 'He Was a Thief'. In 'Bahadur', when the servant-boy Bahadur runs away from his employment after being repeatedly beaten, the housewife Nirmala and other members of the family repent on their conduct. She reasons that had Bahadur stolen something, she would have felt content with him running away. The fact that he left behind even his meagre possessions together with all the salary he had earned made her feel acutely guilty. The upright servant shook up the moral certitude of his employers.

One strong sketch which appears in varying ways in these stories is the power of irony: servants live amidst the material objects of comfort which are not meant for them. In 'The Whip of Fortune', Nathua could not resist trying the king-size spring bed in the house where he worked. On doing so, he was caught and beaten badly, which forced him to run away and transform into a person who eventually returned to sleep on that very same bed, as a rich and accomplished man. The lure of comfort and the reality of dejection is the perennial conflict with which servants live their entire lives. In the plenitude of objects that provide comfort, their desires remain invisible. The objects that they clean and are required to keep safe, they otherwise cannot 'touch' and use. Being so proximate and yet unbelievably distant is the fundamental irony of their lives.

The most potent way of invisibilizing the servant is through sexuality. Here, on this matter, the literary representation appears to be highly gendered. Women domestics are the 'objects' of lust and hence a threat to the conjugal life of their employers. In 'Maidservant', Premchand indicates that the mistress of the household is uncomfortable with the presence of the first maid who is quite young. She is eventually fired. In contrast, in the case of male young domestics, who too are generally seen as a 'threat', in 'Blouse' and 'On the Boil', we notice a palpable brewing of confused sexual desire which is not fully comprehensible to even them. While these figures are usually seen as a threat, these two stories ask readers to reconsider that domestic servants, particularly young ones, might also be transitioning in the realm of their desires which they cannot express in their immediate social context. Broadly, while providing care work in other households, the servants' own emotional transitions, requirements and desires often go unnoticed. Overall, these stories foreground servants in the web of intersecting issues and discourses on domesticity, nationalism, class, caste, gender, age, sexuality and other social markers of distinction and subordination.

As we let readers dive into the beauty of these stories, which we have only managed to explain and explore superficially, we think it would suffice to provide in the end just one- or two-sentence descriptions of each of these stories. In a self-effacing and humorous tone, Premchand's 'Maidservant' (महरी, 1936) portrays the centrality of work along the culturally conceived notions of maid and mistress in a middle-class household, and the perils and profits of hiring a maid. His second piece, 'The Whip of Fortune' (सौभाग्य के कोड़े, 1924) is a melodramatic narrative of a brutalized runaway child-servant who ends up becoming a music maestro and marries his (former) master's daughter. Rambriksha Benipuri's 'He Was a Thief' (वह चोर था, 1928–30) is a story of a self-consciously reformist zamindar and his personal attendant, exploring the cultural dilemmas and complexity of the master–servant relationship against the backdrop of a turbulent political climate and infatuations with new egalitarian ideas. His second piece, 'Mangar' (मंगर, 1940–41) is the character sketch of a sturdy ploughman/servant turning old and frail. It is portrayed by the master's son who is a writer and an anti-colonial activist committed to radical egalitarian ideas. 'Sabia' (सबिया, 1935) and 'Rama' (रामा, 1930) are also sketches of servants' lives penned by Mahadevi Varma – an acclaimed romantic poet, educationist and one of the precursors to modern feminist movements. 'Sabia' is a sweeper-maid, a kind-hearted, hard-working, and caring breadwinner of her family, who refuses to lose her goodness and dignity despite facing betrayal from her disloyal husband. 'Rama' is the life story of Varma's childhood babysitter and the latter's emotional bond with the three children in the house of his employer. These sketches are modern(ist) inversions of a traditional literary aesthetic style, tip-to-toe description (*nakh-shikh varnan*) of beauty, virtues and/or chivalry of ideal heroines/heroes. Jainendra Kumar's 'Ratnaprabha' (रत्नप्रभा, 1944) is a psychologized tale of the relationship between a young male servant and his rich, lonely young mistress. Saadat Hasan Manto's 'Blouse' (ब्लाउज़, 1941) explores the unarticulated emotions of a resident boy-servant going through puberty in a household populated by an elderly master–mistress couple and their young daughters. 'On the Boil' (उबाल, 1941), by Upendra Nath 'Ashk', explores the inchoate psycho-sexual emotions of an orphan youngster who is a full-time domestic servant in a household of a recently wedded couple. Amarkant's 'Bahadur' (बहादुर, 1973) explores the life of a young servant hailing from the hills and serving a middle-class family and dispassionately unpacks the pathology of everyday class violence in such households. And in the end, Shekhar Joshi's debut story, 'Dajyu', (दाज्यु, 1956) explores the making and unmaking of the filial bond between a servant from the hills at a coffeeshop and its regular customer who hails from the same region and is a lonely man in the town. Although not about a domestic servant, through this story a reader can easily sense a continuum in the predicament of a filial bond inside the home and outside.

Deepmala Gupta

Maidservant

PREMCHAND

I

May god bless Lalluji's Ma, whose efforts have made all sorts of comfort possible. Otherwise, is it not a miracle that I have never been late to the office, despite being in the postal services that demands an attendance of seven to eight hours a day? It is as if the household chores themselves take care of finishing on time, saying, 'our train is never late'. Like parts of a clock, every object at home finds its own way of remaining perfectly placed in its position. This is all due to the magic of Lalluji's Ma. If I were asked to go to office on a Sunday, I would cry. And there she is, poor woman, who doesn't care for a Sunday or a Christmas break. The workload keeps on increasing every day. While my vanity swells in proportion to my salary, she doesn't utter a word of complaint. By the grace of the Almighty, there are four children in the house.

Their mammoth responsibility will hardly grant recess to any other woman, yet only god knows how she manages to finish so many other tasks. She attends to all the chores related to my personal comfort. Hot water is ready early in the morning during winters, shaving material is all set, prayer utensils are rinsed, shoes are polished – there is no scope to point a finger of complaint. The most joyous of all facts is that they come at no expense. There was a time when I used to earn a monthly salary of twenty rupees and endured on local shoes and a plain checkered coat. Now, thanks to almighty, I receive hundred rupees a month and I don't settle for anything less than a pair of shining shoes and a silk coat. And she, a poor woman, continues to live the same life as before. An ornament every second year, an annual dip in the holy Triveni, that's all of that makes her more than happy. On the other side are people like us. For us, salary increments arrive annually and yet we whine incessantly. The Postal Association gives calls for annual salary hikes and reductions in office hours, and demands that no higher officer may dare raise his voice at us. It is evident that Lalluji's Ma eats the same *dal–chawal* as I do. But it is for god's blessing that she is always quiet and content and I remain forever impatient and disgruntled.

II

I deposit my entire salary in the hands of Lalluji's Ma and get all the luxuries that are not in the destiny of even those officers who draw a salary of three hundred rupees.

Guests are also happy and so are the relatives. Truth be told, the amount of work she does is worth more than a hundred rupees. Sahibs hire ayahs for their children for a monthly wage of rupees fifteen or twenty, but they are not so lucky to receive the affection and comfort that my kids do. If I employ a cook against a payment of ten rupees plus provide for his food, he would not cook as well as Lalluji's Ma. To top all this, frugality is integral to her outlook. If I hire a personal attendant, he would not be able to manage and look after things better than her. The cost of tailoring kids' clothes comes to a lump sum of ten to fifteen rupees per month. A maid for cleaning and dishwashing would charge another five to ten. That is to say, no matter how you do your calculations, even after I gift my entire earnings to the servants, I would not get the same level of comfort I do because of my goddess lady.

III

Either you call it the impact of English education or of reading newspapers, or the result of the speeches delivered by towering leaders, it often comes to my mind that making the life partner toil so much is awfully oppressive. It is unjust for a woman to work to such an extreme, but poor woman, she doesn't ask for anything on her own. Possibly, the idea to think about her own comfort does not strike her. At times I feel a strong urge to hire a maid to alleviate her drudgery. It is indeed very selfish that I, acting like a Babu, avail all kinds of pleasures and the goddess of my home toils endlessly like a maidservant. But whenever I discuss the issue with Deviji (Lalluji's Ma), she laughs it off.

'Why do you want to needlessly increase expenses? I am not an educated woman, who would keep lying on the bed throughout the day or go for a walk in the mornings and evenings. Let things run just the way they are.' If I put pressure, she goes on to say, 'I am not stopping you, hire a maid if you so wish.'

Before my guardianship, there was always a maid in the house. I often remember those old days. After the old woman Nauli departed, the house has had no maid. May god bless her; her back had bent, but she did all the work alone until her death. She always served; she never received any care or service even when she fell ill. The icing on the cake was this: she worked for a rupee plus food. And she died leaving behind her lifetime's earnings in our home. Serving better than a mother, she was the one who shared our grief and pain. Where do you find such a servant these days? What a wonderful time it was, people were prosperous despite low wages. On the contrary, nowadays both income and expenditure have increased, yet there is an unceasing discontentment all the time. Earlier every commodity was cheap. *Lattha* as well as high-quality muslin cost four annas a *gaz*, the finest sweets five-six annas per *ser*. Now expenses have doubled, but the erstwhile quality and finesse are hard to find. May god turn the clock back, even if for a short duration. At least once there should be the joy of abundance at rock-bottom prices.

IV

Then I vowed to hire a maid, neither due to requirement nor due to anyone's advice, but because it was fashionable and so I wished for it. But this resolution did not end well. I could not relish this undertaking. On each occasion I faced new problems; forget comfort, it in fact became a constant source of worry. There began the daily disappearance of clothes and utensils. Expenses spiked. If earlier, for example, ghee worth fifteen rupees lasted a month, its consumption now rose to cost twenty-five. The maid would wax lyrical about her previous master, 'This is how exuberant things were there; that is how lavish it was there; this much of ghee flowed there into the kitchen sink; dishes were done with milk; this much I got; that much I was paid.'

In sum, less comfort and more spending, and in addition came unceasing squabbles.

V

The first maid who came might have been twenty to twenty-two years of age. You cannot probably call her pretty, but she was definitely very polite and had a kind of glow in her eyes. Although nothing significant ever happened, Deviji always had complaints. She commented that now I went late to work and came back early. I, however, stayed in the office for the full hours required of me. What is timely or late in a post office job? Another complaint she made was that I stared too much at Jamna (the maidservant) and that I kept talking to her all the time. But I didn't feel unusual about it. But, eventually, when the increasing number of complaints took the shape of grief and mourning, I dismissed Jamna from the job. Afterwards, I deliberately searched for and employed an old woman so that any possibility of distrust within the home did not arise and the need for extra help also got fulfilled. This experiment, however, was also a failure. The old woman could neither carry a vessel of water nor move a bed. She was like a bag of skin and bones, and, truthfully, she in fact should have had a servant for herself. Be that as it may, Lalluji's Ma could not get any respite in spite of the maid's presence. She toiled as much as she did before. But, meanwhile, I made a fool of myself. In a nutshell, I also relieved the old lady from her service, and then began the search for a middle-aged woman. Through a 'Service Seeking Agency' a forty-year-old maid was found. Before her, many maids had come and gone. One had asked for the details of work, and when the specifics were given, she left commenting that the task was equivalent to the work of two servants, but the wages didn't even match for one. So, when the next maid came, I told her that there was hardly any work, all she was required to do was to keep lying on the bed. She also left. This whole situation was odd. If work is assigned, the servant doesn't stay. If I said there was hardly any work, then also there was no success. However, after searching for a week or a fortnight, another maid was found who could neither be suspected of being too young or beautiful, nor was she shy of hard work. After a long deliberation, I hired her for the job.

VI

In some time, we discovered that this woman was erratic – at times she worked quite well, but other times she did not do anything at all. What is more, she behaved rudely at will. Listen to this incident: one day, on finding some imprints of fingers on a plate, Deviji said, 'Champa, this plate is very dirty.' Champa replied, 'These are the marks of a clean palm and fingers. Anyone can see that. And anyway these are not mine; must be Huma's (my elder daughter). Children play with mud and soil in this family.'

Deviji: 'Hey, Champa, why do you lie so much? Does the girl have such big fingers? You concoct hopeless stories and malign the children.'

Champa: 'I only make stories, but you are the one who deals in lies.'

Deviji: 'Mind your language. We will fire you at the end of this month.'

Champa: 'I will myself quit in a few days, who are you to fire me? I was waiting for the right opportunity. My man is surprised how I even manage to work for so long in this house. No servant can survive here. Every petty thing is locked and sealed. Only a bare wage. It is amply clear that no servant has ever worked here.'

As I returned from office that evening, I heard about the exchange. I ignored and coldly suggested to Deviji to fire the maid if she so wished. Later, I was really repentant of the injustice I did to Lalluji's Ma. However, I admonished Champa and the incident was soon forgotten. This continued as usual for some time.

VII

Listen to another incident: Deviji called out for Champa a dozen times. She was downstairs, but did not reply. Champa hears perfectly well but has the habit of not replying. Deviji came downstairs and asked her, 'I have called you a hundred times, but you didn't reply!'

Champa: '*Arey Bibi*, excuse me, please don't lie. You called only a dozen times but counted a hundred. You yourself had said that you would dismiss me at the end of the last month, and today is the first day of the new month. Why should I respond now?'

Deviji left fuming with anger. Champa's responses, like electricity, were quick and jolting, but poor Deviji, who lived in purdah, had no option but to swallow her anger and stay silent, partly also because of me. She did not even complain to me. If my room was not well cleaned and if she reminded Champa about the same, the latter would retort, 'As if it was very clean earlier!' One day, Champa broke two porcelain vases. When Deviji enquired, she said, 'The kids broke them.'

Deviji: 'The boys don't ever touch them.'

Champa: 'Okay! Yes, my mistress, I broke them. When was I told not to break the vases? You'd mentioned glass utensils, and so, not a single piece of them has ever broken till now. It is certain that one who works may unwittingly also damage things. The vases were pretty old anyway ... You don't want a servant, so you keep making senseless and false allegations.'

When I reached home in the evening, Champa said, 'Yes, *sarkar*, I committed a mistake. While cleaning, a vase fell over the other and thus they broke.'

I try my best to stay happy. What else could I do – I deal with office rush in the day and domestic hassles in the evening! One day I told her, 'Champa, a pin is peeping out of my shoes – please hammer that in with something.'

She remained silent. Perhaps she was thinking that at the time of hiring, she had not been briefed about such tasks. That is why, probably, she didn't even touch the shoes. Finding the nail in the same state the next morning, I asked her if the pin she had fixed the previous evening had spiked out again. At this, she replied, 'Babuji, the shoes are quite old – how long will they last? Please replace them. And please buy a costly pair so that they last.'

Enduring this for a while, when I finally got fed up with her conduct, I ousted her and never hired a maid again. This is how I have recovered my lost peace effortlessly. It is true, the days of keeping servants are long gone. A man is his best servant.

The Whip of Fortune

PREMCHAND

I

Children, no matter if they are from rich families or poor, are instinctively playful. This exuberance is usually not mindful of their social status and condition. Nathua's parents had died. He was often to be seen dawdling around the precincts of Rai Bholanath's home. Rai Saheb was a compassionate man; once in a while he gave Nathua a few pennies. Leftover food from his house was more than sufficient to feed many such orphans. Nathua also used hand-me-down clothes from Rai Saheb's children. So, he was not unhappy despite being an orphan.

Rai Saheb had freed Nathua from the clutches of a Christian. It hadn't occurred to him that the boy might get a decent education and live comfortably at the mission. It was preferable that he remained a Hindu. Rai Saheb believed that the leftovers from his own home were purer than the food received at the mission. Cleaning his house was more important than the boy's education at the mission school. He should stay a Hindu, regardless of his condition. If he converted to Christianity, he would forever be lost.

Nathua had no work other than sweeping Rai Saheb's bungalow. Once he had eaten, he played and loitered around. His work came handy in assigning him to a certain caste: the servants of the household referred to him as *bhangi* and to this Nathua had no objection. The poor lad hadn't a clue what a name could do to his status. As far as he was concerned, there was no harm in being a bhangi. While sweeping, he would occasionally find money or some other objects of value. He would then use that money to buy cigarettes. In the company of the other servants, he became addicted to smoking, chewing tobacco and paan.

There was no dearth of children at Rai Saheb's house – dozens of nephews and nieces were all around. But he only had one child of his own – a daughter named Ratna. She had two private tutors, including a memsahib who used to come and teach her English. Rai Saheb had a deep wish that Ratna should become an all-accomplished maiden! May she become like Goddess Lakshmi in whosoever's household she might later enter. He did not let her spend time with any other kid and had made two separate rooms for her – a bedroom and a study. It is believed that excessive love makes a child importunate and haughty, yet Ratna was well mannered despite the indulgence showered upon her. She never spoke rudely to a servant or mistreated a beggar. She would give money and sweets to Nathua, which was why the lad had become cheeky and audacious with her.

One day Nathua was cleaning Ratna's bedroom as the girl was studying English with the memsahib in the other room. While sweeping the floor, he felt an urge to lie down on Ratna's bed. What a clean white bedsheet, how soft and thick the mattress, what a beautiful shawl this was! And how comfortably Ratna slept on this bed – like a hatchling in the nest! That's why Ratna's hands were so soft and fair, as though her body were made of cotton.

Thinking that hardly anyone watched over there, the unfortunate boy wiped his feet on the floor, quickly lay on the bed, and then pulled the shawl over himself. His heart was beaming with joy and pride. Out of excitement, he bounced on the bed a couple of times. He felt as if he was lying on a heap of cotton. Whichever side he turned, his body sank three inches deep into the mattress. 'This heavenly pleasure is not for me,' he thought. 'Why didn't the Almighty make me the son of Rai Saheb?' Such great feelings of pleasure swiftly made him recall his actual condition, and he felt dejected.

All of a sudden, Rai Saheb came into the room out of some necessity. On finding Nathua on Ratna's bed, he exclaimed, 'Hey, you pig! What on earth do you think you are doing?!'

Nathua was filled with such extreme nervousness, as if he had fallen into a river. He jumped out of the bed and stood at a distance; then he picked up the broom.

Rai Saheb asked him again, 'What the hell were you doing?'

'Nothing *sarkar*.'

'You have become so daring that you sleep on Ratna's bed? You ungrateful idiot! Someone bring my *hantar*!'

After getting hold of his hantar, Rai Saheb thrashed Nathua heavily. The poor boy prayed, prostrated himself and begged for forgiveness, but Rai Saheb's anger showed no signs of abatement. All the servants gathered around and started rubbing salt on Nathua's wounds. Rai Saheb's anger kept on soaring. He threw away his hantar and started kicking Nathua. When Ratna heard the commotion, she ran in and, after learning what had transpired, said, 'Dadaji, this poor lad will die; have mercy on him.'

'If he dies, I'll dispose of his body. He should experience the fruits of his own misdemeanour.'

'It was my bed, and I forgive him.'

'Have a look at the state of your bed. It must be filled with the filth off this scoundrel's body. What did he think he was doing?' He turned again to Nathua, 'You rascal! What were you up to?'

Rai Saheb pounced once more, but Nathua hid behind Ratna. Stopping her father, Ratna cried, 'Dadaji, please forgive him at my plea.'

'What are you saying, Ratna? Are such criminals worth clemency? Nevertheless, I shall let him go on your appeal; I would have killed him otherwise. Listen, Nathua! If you know what's good for you, don't ever come back here – get out now, you worthless pig!'

Nathua ran for his life. He did not look back. Only upon reaching the main road, he halted. Here Rai Saheb could not do anything to him. Not everyone out here would be supportive of Rai Saheb's behaviour. At least, somebody would say that he is just a boy. Even if he has committed a blunder, would you really kill him for that? 'Let him beat me here,' thought Nathua, 'I will shout and run away; who can catch me then!' Thinking so, he got some courage in him. He turned his face back towards the bungalow and shouted, 'Come here, I'll see you.' And then he ran onwards, lest Rai Saheb heard him.

II

After he had ran some distance, Nathua saw Ratna's memsahib approaching in a horse-drawn carriage. He thought that she was coming to catch him. He sprinted away again, but stopped when his legs gave away. He reassured himself, 'What would she do to me? What harm have I done to her?' In a moment the memsahib had caught up with him.

'Nathua, where are you going?'

'Nowhere.'

'If you go back to Rai Saheb's, he will beat you. Why don't you come with me? You can live in the mission hostel. You'll become a gentleman.'

'You won't make me become a Christian, will you?'

'Are you crazy? Is a Christian worse than a bhangi?'

'No, no, I will not be a Christian.'

'If you prefer not to, then don't be one. Nobody will make you convert.'

Nathua walked beside the carriage for some time, but he was still suspicious. Suddenly he stopped. The memsahib asked, 'Why don't you keep walking with me?'

'I have heard that whoever goes to the mission becomes a Christian. I won't go. You are bluffing me.'

'You are sorely misled! You will be educated there. You will not be at the service of anyone. Every evening you will be given leave to go and play. You will get new clothes to wear. Come and try it for a couple of days at least.'

Nathua did not reply to this tempting offer. Instead, he ran down a nearby lane. When the horse carriage had moved some distance ahead, he started to think calmly, 'Maybe I should go. What if a policeman arrests me and puts me in the *thana*? People of my caste live there. Will they look after me in their homes? Anyway, I'm not going to sit around idly and eat other people's food; I will work, I'll earn my own bread. Everyone should get some backing from their community, that's all. Had there been someone to cover my back today, Rai Saheb wouldn't have dared batter me like he did. The entire community would have gathered and surrounded him; any cleaning of his household would have ceased for good. Nobody would ever come to sweep his veranda again. All his *Raisahebi* would have dissipated. All that grandeur would have fallen.'

Musing on such ideas, he arrived at the bhangi neighbourhood. It was evening already. Sitting on a mat beneath a tree, some bhangis were playing the *shahnai* and *tabla*. They practised every day – this was their livelihood. Nowhere has the art of music been so badly demeaned as among this group of people! Nathua went and stood nearby. On seeing him attentively listening to the music, one of the bhangis asked, 'Do you sing?'

'No, not yet; if you teach me, I will,' replied Nathua.

'Don't make excuses, sit down; let me know if you have any melody in your voice. Unless it is there, who will teach you?'

Nathua, like any other street kid, knew how to sing a bit. While walking through the market he used to sing songs. So he started singing at once. The master listened to him. He was a gem-finder in this art of music; he recognized that the boy was not an ordinary piece of glass but a diamond. 'Where do you live?' he asked.

Nathua narrated his epic story; the acquaintance was made. He was given shelter and, moreover, an opportunity, which elevated him from the ground to the stars.

III

Three years flew by. Nathua's singing caused great excitement in the town. He did not have just one quality but was a treasure house of talent. Singing, playing shahnai, *pakhavaj*, *sarangi*, *tambura*, *sitar* – he mastered all the instruments. The maestros, too, wondered about the provenance of his magical wisdom. It seemed as if he was simply revising an already studied art. Many would try to learn sitar for more than ten years, yet fail to become adept, but Nathua could find his way around its strings in only a month's time. Many such jewels abound, but they go to waste because they miss out on the chance of a rendezvous with the jeweller.

It was sheer coincidence that one day there was a music festival in Gwalior. Musical maestros from all over the country and beyond were invited. Master Ghure was also going to be present and Nathua was his disciple. The master left for Gwalior and took Nathua along with him. There was massive fanfare in Gwalior for a week and Nathua earned a tremendous reputation. He received a gold medal in recognition of his skills. The president of the Gwalior Music School requested that Master Ghure get the boy admitted. He would receive a general education along with training in music. Ghure was quick to concur and Nathua agreed as well.

In five years, Nathua attained the highest degree available at the school. His intelligence was reflected in his passion for the disciplines of languages, mathematics and the sciences too. Now, he was an asset to society. Nobody bothered to ask him which caste he belonged to. His lifestyle, manners and demeanour were no longer those of a humble singer but of the educated gentry. To protect his dignity, he started conducting himself like a high-caste man. He gave up meat and alcohol and started performing evening prayers regularly. Not even a noble Brahmin could match him in his conduct. His name was Nathua, but as he grew more refined he became famous as N. R. Acharya. Usually people called him 'Acharya' (the maestro). He started receiving a handsome salary from the royal court. It is rare that any man of distinction is blessed with so much fame at the tender age of eighteen. But fame is an unquenchable thirst; akin to the legendary Vedic sage Agastya, it is never sated even after drinking an entire ocean. And so, the honourable Acharya left for Europe – he wished to master Western music, too. He entered the most prestigious music school in Germany and, after five years of hard work, he returned to Gwalior via Italy with the title of 'maestro'. Barely after a week, Madan Theatre Company appointed him as supervisor of its various branches on a salary of ₹3,000, a princely sum in those days. He had already saved up thousands of rupees before going to Europe. And he had been warmly welcomed to the opera houses and theatres of Europe, where a day's earnings sometimes exceeded what the greatest singers in India would make in years. Because of his extraordinary love for Lucknow, Nathua decided to reside there.

IV

When the honourable Acharya got to Lucknow, his heart was glowing with joy. It was here that his childhood had been spent. He was an orphan once, flying kites in the same streets and begging for money it is very markets. It is here he was whipped; the scars were visible even now. Yet these marks were more meaningful to him than the lines of fortune on his hands – his whipping had proved to be Shiva's boon. He bore no anger or bad feeling in his heart for Rai Saheb. The latter's ills were forgotten; only virtues remained in Acharya's memory, and Ratna rose up in his mind as a compassionate womanly figure. Crisis aggravates old wounds, prosperity heals them. When Acharya alighted from the train, his heart was pounding. That child of ten years was now a twenty-three-year-old educated gentleman. Even his mother would not have recognized her own Nathua. However, the city's transformation was more surprising than the changes in his personality. It was not Lucknow anymore; it was some other place.

As soon as he got out of the station, he saw a huge crowd waiting to welcome him. One of them was a young woman who resembled Ratna. People shook hands with him and the woman threw garlands around his neck. This was a reward for making India famous abroad. Acharya's legs were trembling, he felt that he could no longer stand – why, it was the very same Ratna! That innocent girl was now an idol of beauty, honour, pride and modesty. He hardly had the courage to make eye contact with her.

After greeting the crowd, he entered a well-adorned bungalow. He was surprised to see that it was the very same one where he had played with Ratna; there were the same accoutrements, pictures, furniture, mirrors – even the floor was exactly the same. On stepping inside, Acharya felt the same way a pious Hindu would upon entering a temple. On reaching Ratna's old bedroom, he felt a wrench in his heart and tears came forth. It was the same bed and bedspread, and the very floor that he used to sweep! He asked excitedly, 'Who is the owner of this bungalow?'

The manager of the theatre company was with him, and he replied: 'It belongs to one Rai Bholanath.'

'Where did Rai Saheb go?' questioned Acharya.

'Only god knows about his whereabouts. This bungalow was auctioned off due to his debts. We found that it was very close to our theatre, so we corresponded with the officials and purchased it for the company. The bungalow, including all its fixtures and fittings, was bought for forty thousand rupees.'

'Goodness, you got it for practically nothing! Is there really no news of Rai Saheb?'

'I heard that he went on a pilgrimage, god only knows if he returned.'

When Acharya was sitting quietly in the evening, he asked a man passing by, 'Hey, do you know Master Ghure? I've heard a lot about him.'

The man replied sadly, 'Sir, don't ask about him. He was walking home drunk and fell down in the middle of the road. A truck was coming from the other side. The driver could not see him and the truck ran him over. His body was found in the morning. He was the only one of his kind; all of Lucknow is a desert now, and there is nobody in the city to be proud of. He trained a boy named Nathua and we also had some hopes in him in keeping the legacy of his master alive, but he went to Gwalior and after that no one has any idea where he vanished.

V

The honourable Acharya lived in the bungalow like a new bride at her in-laws' home. Old predispositions refused to die. His soul repudiated the reality that it was his house now. He often felt startled in the middle of his laughter. When friends dined, he experienced unfathomable doubts. He could not sleep in the study; the idea was deeply entrenched in him that this room was for study alone. He could not bring himself to replace the old things in the house with new and better ones. And he hardly ever opened the door to Ratna's bedroom. His legs would tremble upon entering the room, and he never even thought of lying on the bed.

Acharya displayed the magic of his musical accomplishment many times at the university in Lucknow. He had vowed to stop performing in the houses of the wealthy and powerful, even if they offered to pay him millions. People hugely enjoyed listening to his incredible and otherworldly music.

One day when Acharya got up after his morning prayers, Rai Bholanath came to see him. Ratna also accompanied him. The honourable Acharya felt overwhelmed – his heart had never been so moved, even at the huge theatres in Europe. He bowed before Rai Saheb. His humility made Bholanath somewhat nervous. Long ago people used to bow before him; now he was the subject of ridicule everywhere he went. Ratna, too, felt ashamed. Gazing in the other direction, the humbled Rai Saheb asked, 'Do you like this place?'

'Oh, yes, I can't imagine a place better than this,' Acharya answered.

Bholanath then said, 'This is my bungalow. I made it and then unmade it too.'

Ratna spoke shyly, 'Dadaji, what's the use of such chatter?'

'If there is no use, there is no loss either. Sharing my troubles with the gentleman comforts my soul.' He went on, 'Sir, this is my bungalow – rather, it *was* mine. My income from land revenue was once fifty thousand per annum. In the company of some bad sorts, I got addicted to gambling. Upon winning a couple of good rounds, I became more adventurous. I started playing for millions, but in one defeat I lost everything. The bet was for twenty five lakh rupees; had I won this bungalow would have been made fuller with splendour. Now I regret the good old days. My Ratna is a great lover of your music. She talks about you often. I have educated her to bachelor's level ...'

Ratna's face turned red with shame, and she exclaimed, 'Dadaji, the Honourable Acharya knows my situation, he does not need all these details.' Then she turned to Acharya, 'Sir, please forgive us. My father has become unstable in his mind after that financial loss. He came with an appeal that he would like to visit the bungalow sometimes, unless you have any objection. This would give him solace. He would be consoled with the fact that a friend owns it. We have come to visit merely to communicate this plea.'

Acharya replied politely, 'There is no need for my permission. This is your house, please come whenever you wish. In fact, you can stay here if you want. I will find some other place for myself.'

Rai Saheb thanked him and left. He would then return almost every other day and spend hours at the bungalow. Ratna also accompanied him regularly. Then he started coming daily.

One day, in private, Rai Saheb asked Acharya, 'Excuse me, but why don't you call your family and children here? You must be uncomfortable alone.'

Acharya replied, 'I am not married yet, and I don't want to be.' He lowered his gaze.

'But why, what enmity do you have with marriage?'

'I can't give a particular reason, it is just a wish.'

'Are you a Brahmin?'

Acharya was taken aback. He replied in a doubtful voice, 'Caste distinction becomes null and void after travelling to Europe. Whatever I might be by birth, I am surely a Shudra through my vocation.'

'Then hail your humility. That such great men are still found in this world! I also believe in the *varna* that comes from *karma*. Politeness, modesty, humility, manners, religiosity, love for education – all these are the qualities of a Brahmin, and I believe you *are* a Brahmin. Ratna loves you a great deal. No suitor has ever appealed to her before, but you have hypnotized her. I am sorry for troubling you; your parents …'

'You are like both my parents. I don't know who I was born to. They died when I was too young.'

'If they were alive, they would be so proud of you. Where can one find such a virtuous son?'

In the meantime, Ratna came in with a piece of paper and told Rai Saheb, 'Dadaji, the Honourable Acharya is also a poet, I have picked this up from his desk. Except for the work of Sarojini Naidu, I have never read poetry like this.'

Acharya stole a glance at Ratna and said shyly, 'I had just scribbled some stray words. What would I know of poetry?'

VI

Both were enamoured and in love. Ratna was enchanted by the musician's artistry and Acharya was enthralled by her love. Had she not been there at the station when he returned to Lucknow, he would not have been acquainted with her again! But who is not attracted to the open invitation of love? Is there a heart that cannot be conquered so?

Acharya was now confronted with a dilemma. His heart spoke, 'The moment my truth is revealed to her, Ratna will surely turn away from me. No matter how liberal she is or how terribly she feels about the shackles of caste, she cannot be free from the hatred for me that will then come naturally.' So, he did not have the courage to unveil his real identity. 'Oh! It may not have mattered much if she only felt hatred. But she will be sad and will be in great pain; her heart will be shattered; heaven knows what she would do to herself in such a state.' Affirming the bond of love while keeping Ratna in darkness, he felt, was a repugnant act of the first order. It was deceit, a form of infidelity. It was cunning; it was strictly forbidden in love. Because of such a quandary, he felt indecisive.

At the same time, Rai Saheb's visits were on the rise. His words always reflected what was in his mind. Ratna's visits were now less frequent. And this made Rai Saheb's thoughts even more explicit. Three or four months passed. Acharya took to pondering along the lines, 'It's the same Rai Saheb who thrashed me and kicked me out of this house for lying on Ratna's bed for a few moments. If he ever found out that I am the same orphan, untouchable, homeless child, how self-tortured, ashamed, humiliated and repentant would he feel!'

One day, Rai Saheb announced, 'The wedding date should be finalized. I want to get rid of this sacred debt.'

Despite knowing very well what he meant, Acharya asked, 'What date?'

Rai Saheb replied, 'Ratna's wedding. I don't believe in horoscopes, but a wedding has to be on an auspicious date.'

Acharya looked at the ground without saying anything.

'You know my condition,' Rai Saheb went on, 'I am no longer useful for anything except marrying off my daughter. Save Ratna, I have no reason to be here at all.'

Acharya was lost in his thoughts.

Rai Saheb spoke once more: 'You know Ratna yourself. My eulogy is meaningless. Whether good or bad, you have to accept her.'

Acharya's eyes welled up with tears.

'I completely believe that the gods have sent you here only for her,' explained Rai Saheb. 'I beg of the Almighty that both of you live happily forever. To me, there can't be anything more blissful than this. After I am released from this duty, I wish to devote myself to prayer and worship. Indirectly, you will also reap the fruits of my pious deeds.'

Acharya replied as he choked on his emotions, 'You are like a father to me, but I am not at all suitable for her.'

Rai Saheb embraced him and said, 'My son, you are the most accomplished man. You are the jewel of society. It would really be an honour for me if I got a son-in-law like you. I shall finalize the wedding date today and inform you by tomorrow.'

He stood up after saying this. Acharya wanted to say something more, but did not get the chance, or perhaps he did not have the courage.

VII

A month passed after the wedding. Ratna's arrival had illuminated her husband's household and purified his heart. It was as if lotuses were blooming in the ocean.

One evening after dinner, Acharya was reclining on the same bed that had caused him to be ousted from the house and changed his destiny all those years ago.

For over a month he had been looking for the opportunity to reveal his secret to Ratna. Crushed under the weight of his past and predispositions, his heart was not ready to accept that his fortunes were the outcome of his talent. As if, he was trying to judge the purity of his coins by melting them in a furnace. But he did not get the right opportunity. The moment Ratna was around him, he felt captivated by her presence. Isn't it the case that a person needs a dark chamber to cry alone? One does not go to a garden to do so.

Ratna entered smiling. She dimmed the lamps.

Smiling too, Acharya asked, 'Should I turn off the light now?'

Ratna said, 'Why do you feel shy of me?'

'Yes, I am indeed bashful.'

'Because I won you over?'

'No, because I betrayed you.'

'You don't have the ability to betray.'

'You don't know. I have deceived you badly.'

'I know everything.'

'Do you know who I am?'

'Yes, very well. I have known you for a long time. When you and I played in the same garden, I used to beat you and you would cry; I gave you my leftover sweets and you pounced on them. Even then I loved you; yes, love was very much there, but in the form of pity.'

In his great surprise, Acharya asked: 'Ratna, despite knowing this ...'

'Yes, I knew it, that is why I did it. Had I not, I would not have married you.'

'It's the same bed.'

'And I have come as a bonus on it.'

Embracing her, Acharya whispered, 'You are the goddess of forgiveness.'

'I am your disciple,' Ratna replied.

'Does Rai Saheb know, too?'

'No, he doesn't know. Don't ever tell him, he will commit suicide otherwise.'

'I still remember those whippings.'

'Now my father has nothing to offer in expiation. Are you still not content?'

He Was a Thief

RAMBRIKSHA BENIPURI

I

After reaching the prison, Lakshmi Babu felt that jail, the very idea of which used to rattle him, was not such a terrifying place after all. His well-wishers and friends were sad and his wife kept sobbing tears filling in her eyes. By the grace of Gandhi Baba, patriotism has become an easy thing now – wear khadi, donate, if possible, spin the *charkha* at will, and once in a blue moon, if there is an opportunity, go and get blessed with a couple of playful dives into the Ganga of prison. In the same way, thanks to Gandhi's divine power, this jail is no longer like the old prisons, where flogs rained and fetters clanked, where, in the name of food, a penal diet was given and for sleep, dark cells were offered. Now, the world of the jail has become wonderful. Granted that Lakshmi Babu's big bungalow, that drawing room, those carpets, sofas, the cooks and the silver cutlery are not available here. But whatever is available is sufficient for the survival of any gentleman. He is a political prisoner of 'A' division. There is a set of facilities provided by the government. On top of that it has also allowed these prisoners to add to their comfort by making private arrangements for food and other matters of daily lifestyle.

The room that was allotted to Lakshmi Babu was decorated by him in such a way that within a few days of his arrival, it served as his 'miniature' bungalow. His *rasoiya* was slowly turning into a *bawarchi*; he had already started addressing his *pania* as *bera.*[1] At times, Lakshmi Babu wondered, Alas! If only the jailer were to allow my wife to visit one day, I would have shown her how wrong her impression about the prison was. Whenever the wretched woman visits, she cries and wears a long face, thus spoiling all the fun of the experience. She imagines the conditions prevailing inside the jail by seeing the thick iron rods of the prison gate, its huge locks, and bayonets of the sentinels standing outside! How will she know that the heaven is across the Vaitarni!

After the arrangements of living and accommodation were completed, his highness turned his attention towards reading and writing. A strange epidemic of studying had spread all over the jail, and it seemed to be contagious. He was also doomed to get infected; in fact, he did get infected. And anyway, why should he allow himself to be left behind in any matter? Everyone is studying, so will he. In association with some studious mates, he prepared a list of books, and within a few days his bookshelf was illuminated with books in golden covers.

Since his college days, Lakshmi Babu had hardly enjoyed reading books. After the burden of taking care of his family, business and zamindari fell on his shoulders; when did he have the time to look at books? But this time when he came across them in prison, what was left to be said! He pounced on them and found them exhilarating! As if a plate full of delicious food had been placed before a long-starving person. He turned page after page during the day and even at night; notepad after notepad was coloured with his scribbles. He debated with his comrades on the content of the books over a cup of tea and during evening walks. Until late at night, his lantern remained lit. If the allotted amount of kerosene at the prison was insufficient, he even indulged in manipulations (but only for this noble purpose).

While people read on every subject in jail – from the science of breeding silkworms to Einstein's Theory of Relativity – the most popular subject proved to be socialism. Why would Lakshmi Babu deprive himself of knowing about it? He started studying and contemplating on it in full swing. Yes, not only studying but contemplating as well. And, the contemplation made him realize that for the welfare of society, for the establishment of peace and bliss in the world, socialism was badly needed. But the big question was how to bring about socialism? Isn't this the point from where all conflicts begin? From here the conflict started. Lakshmi Babu solved this contention for himself. Very easy solution: Rejecting Karl Marx, he made Robert Owen his ideal.

Robert Owen! What a simple, saintly figure! Despite being a rich man, he dedicated himself to the upliftment of the poor. Unlike Marx he did not instigate conflict, did not destroy the peace of this troubled world; on the contrary, he tried to create a new world through sacrifice and love. What an ideal his 'New Lanark Colony' was – a human endeavour to build a heaven on earth! If some saints like Owen were born in each country, the world would be redeemed. While contemplating on all this, Lakshmi Babu felt himself to be like Owen, and he imagined in a village under his zamindari he had established one such colony, which was visited by people from across the country. His admiration was in everyone's mouth; columns after columns in the newspapers were filled with admiration for his efforts.

The colony, to which he will give the beautiful Indian name *ashram*, would start later. Could anything be done about it while in jail though? Thinking about the possibility and following the aphorism 'the sooner the better', he began working on his plan. His experiment commenced with two people – one, his 'chef', and the other, his 'waiter'. People were surprised to hear him addressing his waiter as 'Laloo Bhai' and using the respectful pronoun 'aap'. The chef was also now 'Ramjan Bhai'. 'Laloo Bhai, please bring my towel.' 'Ramjan Bhai, how long before the food is ready?' No matter how surprised Ramjan and Laloo were after hearing this mode of address, or if his mates considered him pretentious, Lakshmi Babu found soulful peace. Soulful peace and heartfelt bliss.

The provisions of Laloo and Ramjan also improved. Whatever was cooked, it was for the three of them. Sometimes, Lakshmi Babu tasted Laloo's C-class food in order to experience poverty. What is more, he tried probing into their lives as well. Laloo was in for theft, Ramjan for a rape case. Lakshmi Babu trembled over the term 'rape case'; he quivered at the imagination of this ghastly act, although he agreed that it was also a social curse; an individual merely fell or was pushed into it. Ramjan used to be busy in the drudgery of the kitchen work. So that poor soul was hardly free for Babu's enquiry and questioning. But Laloo was always close to him; therefore, he decided to enter into Laloo's life to understand why a man commits theft?

Yes, diagnosis is needed before administering the medicine. He had read about the importance of diagnosis in his books. But personalized knowledge is also required. And when there is no shortage of idle time in jail, and if there is an individual subject available in the form of Laloo on whom research and experiments could be easily carried out, it would be a great mistake to let go of such an opportunity.

II

Laloo was the youngest of his three brothers. His father was a rural farm labourer. After his wedding, he left his parental village and settled in Laloo's mother's village. Laloo's mother was extremely beautiful. His father could not dismiss the youthful invitation of his beautiful wife. He came to live at his in-laws' place. He was a well-built man who earned well. He ran his household pretty well. He worked in his master's field. He earned sufficient wages to feed his wife and himself. He did some sharecropping too. He reared a cow and a few goats as well. Gradually, he had three sons and a daughter. With the income from his wage, sharecropping, cow and goats, he not only raised his children well but also married them off.

Laloo was married. Soon after his marriage, however, discord started at his house. Both his elder brothers were estranged from the parents. They alleged that the old man loved his youngest son more and was partial towards him. Laloo was not like his father; he not only inherited his facial features and complexion from his beautiful mother but also his physical build. Therefore, he was never able to perform much of the hard work. As the sun glared, he sweated profusely. As the westerly wind blew in winter, his teeth chattered. The old man assigned him a lighter workload. When the brothers got annoyed over their father's partiality, the latter himself tried completing Laloo's share of work. His strength even in that old age was beyond description – he performed work equivalent to two young, physically abled men. When Laloo was reminiscing about his father to Lakshmi Babu, tears were rolling down his face.

Laloo's wife was also very beautiful. When the wife came in his life, he simply hovered around her. He paid no attention to work at all. This became unbearable for his brothers. Finally, they separated from each other – both brothers established their own households; the father took the burden of Laloo upon himself. As long as the old man was alive, Laloo did not even know the distinction between day and night. But an old man is like a ripened mango. One day the mango fell off the tree and the branch was bereft. Laloo was at a loss to understand how he would survive now.

Man is a prisoner of circumstances! Now Laloo was compelled to face the hardships that the real world had in store. His wife encouraged him a lot to face the difficulties headlong. After waking him up in the morning and feeding him leftovers – roti and pickle, bhaat soaked in water, or jaggery – she sent him away for work. She meticulously processed and cooked cereals received in lieu of wages and carried food and beverages to feed him in the field. On her way back she cut grass to feed and maintain the cattle and goats. On Laloo's return in the evening, she washed his feet with affection and she never went to bed before massaging his body with mustard oil.

Her beauty started fading gradually due to this drudgery. For this reason, Laloo felt very aggrieved. What could the poor man do about it? In fact, he himself had lost his previous shining complexion and glow of the skin. While earlier he used to comb his hair daily, now he hardly even looked in the mirror. One day when he was standing in front of a big mirror in the outhouse of the lord, he was shocked to see his full image. Oh, what had he become! Dark complexion, sunken cheeks, and unkempt hair – he could not stand there anymore.

Yet he was contented; somehow, he was managing his life. Neither did he have to shamefully spread his hands out to his brothers for help, nor did his wife need to bear the taunts of his brothers' wives. On the contrary, both were praised for how well they had managed their lives after Laloo's father's passing. He may have appeared a little frivolous in his father's shadow, so what? If he were not to enjoy his life whilst his father was alive and working, when could he have?

But this sense of contentment was not to last for long. The household expanded. The first child brought in joy and bliss. When his wife came out of the maternity home with their first baby girl, Laloo's joy was boundless. The second child was a son – his joy persisted. When every year a child started filling his wife's lap, and his small house became filled with five children within six years, his happiness was replaced by anxiety. When children could hardly be brought up well, who was to ask of their mother's health? The poor woman was wearing out. Gradually, the goats and calves were sold and, finally, the cow. The silver and metallic ornaments, which his aged father had gifted to his daughter-in-law with affection, were also sold one by one. Children became the cause of hunger in the house. Yes, the same kids, who are considered to be the source of joy in the rich households, became the source of starvation in Laloo's hut!

Laloo, despite labouring hard day and night, was unable to push ahead the wheels of domesticity. Did hunger leave any strength in him to perform his best? He was at deep sea without a boat or a rudder. He had no strength left in his hands and limbs to swim across the ocean (of hunger). Suddenly, a rotten corpse came floating his way. He clung to that and started plying forward.

Rotten corpse – the profession of thievery, rotten corpse – stenchful, nuseatic! He was petrified. But what was the alternative? Either he drowned, or he kept holding onto this rotten corpse. Had he been living alone and single, he would never have chosen this occupation – he would rather have died. But, there were these kids and his wife who happened to be a beautiful and lovely woman. He decided to cross the unfathomable ocean, holding onto the rotten corpse.

It was the month of Agahan. The fields were filled with ripe golden-yellow paddy. The farmers' barns were stocked with bundles of crops. Anywhere you looked, it was just grain and grain – ripe, robust, nutritious grains! And, in the midst of such abundance, starvation plagued Laloo's home! One night he could not sleep. His hungry kids were crying incessantly; the mother, exhausted, slapped them on and off, for asking for food. Laloo's stomach growled in hunger. He got up and went out of the house. Stars were shining in the clear sky – like the balance of justice, three stars in a queue were leaning towards the west. The wind was hissing. In the sleepy dead of night, the standing golden paddy in the field were swaying in the rhythm of the breeze. Paddy in the field, and restiveness in the grain-starved abode! What to do? Laloo's mind had stopped working. Involuntarily, his legs moved, hands grabbed the sickle and, trembling all along, he reached the field. He looked around; no one was there, but his hands appeared to be paralysed. He was unable to hold the sickle properly. Somehow, he gripped a handful of paddy and applied his sickle. He was himself surprised at the scraping noise of the dry straw. However, slowly the illusion went away, and so did his hesitation. The hand started functioning, the sickle began working. His sickle was now slicing through the paddy swiftly. Very quickly he entered his courtyard with a bundle of panicles and woke up his wife. He dragged her to the courtyard and said, 'Thrash them and extract the grain right away.'

'Where did it come from? Did you steal?'

Before his wife could shout, he put his hand over her mouth and said, 'If you shout now, I will be caught, beaten up and put in the jail. Just quietly thresh the paddy and keep the grain; warm yourself by burning the straw.'

This is what had happened. With tears in her eyes, his wife took the paddy inside. As the straw burnt, Laloo saw tears flowing from her eyes. He was not less ashamed. But Laloo's shame and his wife's tears were transformed into laughter and joy in the morning when they ate to the full and watched the kids giggling.

Theft? Such an abominable act! When someone is in deep sleep! Taking undue advantage of sleep, an unprecedented gift of nature, lifting grains from some one's barn, breaking his grain store and carrying away sacks of grain, burgling his home and raiding cash and jewellery! Oh, what a ghastly act! But how easy as well! No labour, no drudgery – only some courage is required. Do the magic once and live in comfort with your family for weeks and months. Good returns without any investment.

Over time, Laloo graduated into a seasoned thief. From field to barn, from barn to veranda, from veranda to women's quarters, his reach spread everywhere. While earlier his legs shook, body trembled, breathing heightened, nerves dried, now he was confident and proud of his artful skill. Gradually, he got acquainted with 'senior' thieves. He tutored some new people. Now, he had his own gang.

Big thefts were executed. The village zamindar became his partner – he stored stolen items, sold them and distributed them as per his whims. From constable to inspector, a tacit understanding was established with everyone! Once again, the dupatta began shining on Laloo's wife, his kids chuckled in colourful clothes, beginning with toddy he went up to ganja! Once he had bhang in his childhood and had fallen unconscious from laughing. His father had scolded him badly. From that day on, he had vowed never to indulge in any intoxication. But what should he do now? Gods of the thieves do not get pleased without the offerings of such intoxicants. And could a thief even survive a day if his god is angry? Indulge in intoxication, steal and stay in bliss.

Villagers knew the source of Laloo's indulgence. But who would dare speak? The zamindar had his back and the chowkidar was his partner. On the contrary, now everyone was afraid of Laloo. Everyone feared what would happen if he chose to loot their houses.

But Laloo was saying:

'Babu! Sin cannot be covered. You have to suffer for your misdeeds. Friends are there in good times, but no one cares when misfortunes hit. Once I was caught on the wrong foot, no one cared. Darogaji thrashed me, the chowkidar testified against me and, to my utter surprise, the zamindar nonchalantly digested my share of the booty. My poor wife prayed: "Please help a little; I will fight the case for his release." She ran around the court. She spent whatever was left in the house, but my bad luck caught up. I have been in prison for three years.'

Lakshmi Babu noticed that the tears in Laloo's eyes were tears of repentance. Circumstances had forced him into this filth. His reform was still possible. God and Satan both live in a man's heart. Satan, in this case, certainly triumphed over god, but the latter was immortal. It's the same godliness which was shining in his tears. In nurturing this godliness further and making it victorious within him, Lakshmi Babu would help the pitiable Laloo. He would show the world that a thief can also lead the life of a saint.

III

Lakshmi Babu did not do less for Laloo. When he was released before time as a result of the Gandhi–Irvin Pact, he deposited some money for Laloo at the prison gates. He had taken Laloo's address beforehand. When Laloo's wife sent a letter to prison that someone had sent ₹25 in his children's name, Laloo immediately realized Lakshmi Babu's act of kindness.

At the time of leaving the prison, Lakshmi Babu had said to Laloo, 'Come to my house after your release, I will keep you with me.' Lakshmi Babu had written a few times after his release to Laloo in prison. Initially, the letters had arrived every fortnight, and then later they had arrived with delays. The delay then further elongated; Laloo had received the last letter from Lakshmi Babu after an interval of three months. But was it of any less significance to Laloo that his Babu still remembered him? Earlier, he had decided that after completing his sentence he would first pay a visit to Lakshmi Babu and then go and meet his wife and children. However, affection dragged him back to his village first. After spending a week with his family, he went straight to Lakshmi Babu's house.

Lakshmi Babu had engrossed himself in managing the family and business. He still talked about Owen and discussed socialism with his friends, but Owen's work and ideals of socialism had submerged into his worldly engagements. The village, in which he had vowed to establish an ashram, still had his *kacheri*, where his *amlahs* harangued his tenants and cultivators in a variety of ways for taxes. Yeah, but to compensate, Lakshmi Babu went to his kacheri once a year, called for all his tenants to come in and distributed sweets amongst their children, and in lieu of his pleasant conversation with them wrested a heavy amount as *nazrana*. It was his way of doing 'mass contact'! Imposing his authority on his fellow zamindars, he encouraged them to follow this kind of generosity.

On seeing Laloo, Lakshmi Babu did not feel the same joy, which he had imagined he would while he was in prison. For, now there was no scope left to experiment on Laloo. While he earlier wished to make him a resident of the ashram, Laloo now lived like a servant in his shelter. This much of his benevolence was certainly enough for Laloo! Laloo could not have forgotten his previous beneficence. Laloo devoted himself to the service of Lakshmi Babu with all his body and mind, much like an indebted slave would.

The world of prison is unique. There a man indulges in a variety of phantasms, constructs palaces out of imagination. But in the sirocco of the real world, the same palace collapses like a house of cards. Lakshmi Babu himself was a case in point. He was ready to be the icon of sacrifice in prison, but now he was back into his old luxurious lifestyle. Laloo may also have the same predicament, he thought. Therefore, he kept him as his servant. He was suspicious of him. Hence, to keep a direct watch, he made Laloo his personal attendant. But on getting the opportunity of personal service, Laloo started receiving his maximum affection and benevolence. After testing him on several counts, Lakshmi Babu realized that Laloo had really forgotten his previous life, and was desperately trying to lead a new, pious and austere life. Within a few days, Laloo became Lakshmi Babu's most faithful servant.

One day, a postcard arrived from Laloo's home. The letter first ended up in Lakshmi Babu's hands. After giving the news and condition of his family, Laloo's wife had thanked the new master for his past and present beneficence. And, in the end, she had written to Laloo that his salary of ₹7, which he sent for her monthly expenses, was not sufficient to run the household. Her two children had died. She herself earned a paltry sum as a maid, doing sundry work, such as pounding grain in a Babu's house. However, she wrote, that in this age, maintaining four people was not possible in that amount and, hence, Laloo should pray to his kind master to increase his salary. After reading this letter Lakshmi Babu increased Laloo's salary from ₹7 to ₹10. That night, Laloo couldn't sleep until very late, crushed as he felt under the weight of Lakshmi Babu's gratitude.

Laloo's honesty and devotion progressively brightened like that of the purest gold. Lakshmi Babu's munificence, too, sprouted to the maximum. In the following Phagun, when Laloo was visiting home on fifteen days' leave, Lakshmi Babu gifted a beautiful bordered sari for his wife and printed stitched kurtas for his children. Laloo said to himself: 'Truly, Lakshmi Babu is a god in human form.'

IV

Now, Laloo was not only the most trusted servant of Lakshmi Babu – he kept his suitcase keys, carried his purse and withdrew money from the bank – but also the model representation of Lakshmi Babu's liberality. Whenever any new-age, reform-loving gentleman visited Lakshmi Babu – and they visited quite often – he called Laloo over and extolled him incessantly over his virtues, as if to drive home to them the point about how he had uplifted a fallen life and set him on the righteous path. Truly, if every rich man were to pay attention towards this issue, why would there be theft and robbery in this world, why would jails be filled, why would this world become a living hell? The foundational meaning of *bringing heaven to earth*, about which Jesus spoke, is nothing but the same. Lakshmi Babu thought that even if he could not build an ashram like Owen, so what? Is it a lesser accomplishment to help reform one life? There is a difference between a 'model' and a 'picture'. If an idea from England loses its force and expanse on its way to India, what is so surprising?

One day a Marxian socialist came to Lakshmi Babu's place. In the course of his conversation, Lakshmi Babu delivered a good long lecture on reformism. 'You people only make noise, stir conflict and indulge in destructive activities. You know how to put a house on flames, but not how to construct it. In the clamour of the collective, you do not ever pay attention to an individual. If each one of us takes up the responsibility of one man, many things will change. Do something constructive. Look at my Laloo. He was a thief, his life was dirt. Now he is an honest man. I could not do anything else, but I have the pride of saving one life from ruin, a house from destruction!'

Lakshmi Babu continued in the same vein. The leader was silent for some time. Then, commenting on the futility of such experiments, he said: 'The question of the collective and the individual is very much there. We also have to see how the life of an individual can be made better in this society, and to what extent. You believe Laloo is happy at your place; he is contented with his life. He may feel contented due to his ignorance and prevailing belief. But excuse me, there must have been many moments in his life when the bundle of currency notes in your purse, the beautiful watch on your wrist, your and your family members' shining clothes and ornaments would have caused a pinch, an ache, an anxiety and a desperation in his heart. Laloo may have won them over momentarily, and we may appreciate him for that. But Lakshmi Babu, a day might come when the barrage of his patience will break and the poor man will end up grinding in jail. Granted, one Laloo may spend his full life contended, but there are millions of Laloos, their unquenched desires are intensifying and they are bound to explode one day, therefore it is necessary that society's foundation ...'

But what impact could such arguments leave on Lakshmi Babu? His rant of self-praise went on endlessly. His own life was contented; if he saw or wished to see contentment in everyone's life, why was it so surprising or wrong?

The socialist-Marxist leader had departed and, with him, his words were also gone. The lives of Lakshmi Babu and Laloo continued uninterrupted.

Then, one day, when a director from an insurance company visited Lakshmi Babu, and the latter customarily began praising Laloo, what the director subsequently said made Lakshmi Babu very restless. The director said that one should always beware of men like Laloo. Such men are very conniving. To gain trust, for years they act like the epitome of honesty in front of which the *Ramayana*'s legendary Bharat would also be dwarfed. But later, they filch with such precision that one can only lament not being careful earlier. Their reform is impossible – as Surdas had once said, no other colour can be put over the black colour, so, once a thief, always a thief. He not only said these things as a way of conversation but also proved them with examples that Lakshmi Babu's trust in Laloo was erroneous. Beware! Lakshmi Babu should remain vigilant; lest Lakshmi Babu repents one day that 'there is no use crying over spilt milk' (*phir pachtaye hot kya, jab chidiya chug gayi khet*).

Lakshmi Babu scolded the insurance company director a lot. He kept on thinking after he had left how bizarre such people were. There is always suspicion in their hearts. They always distrust everyone. There is no room for trust. Can the world function without trust? Will, without faith, anyone get trapped in their business of insurance? They will tell others to have faith, but will themselves regard others with suspicion. Amazing is their duplicity! Someone once commits a mistake under duress and then these people keep hauling it over you forever, as if there is no room for improvement in human life.

He was so hurt that he started loving Laloo even more. One day he asked the age of Laloo's eldest child. When Laloo replied that he was already twelve, Lakshmi Babu asked him to bring his eldest and also the younger one when he next visited home. He thought that the elder one would be good for the job of a 'boy' (waiter) for running errands, and he would send the younger one to school. Yes, after educating him, he would show the world how a family could be uplifted from filth and poverty and be made happy and prosperous.

V

'Anything in excess is bad' – Lakshmi Babu's excessive generosity towards Laloo and his family also had one negative repercussion. The other servants became jealous of Laloo. To present Laloo as an item of exhibition, Lakshmi Babu kept him very neat and clean. Gradually, it became his habit. And so, the other servants were envious of Laloo's clean clothes. He bathed with soap, oiled his hair and combed them regularly, too. He had acquired the poise of a Babu. When he had arrived years ago, he mingled with all the servants, sat and chatted with them, sometimes sang and even smoked with them. But now he had started maintaining distance from the rest of the servants. Why would the cohort not be jealous seeing one of them progressing so far and ahead of themselves?

Not only were the servants, even Lakshmi Babu's family members were envious of this pampered servant. When he had arrived, he was always ready to work for everyone. Now, he did not even go near others; he just stuck around Lakshmi Babu. It was not that he had become lazy or idle. In fact, after attending to the personal service of Lakshmi Babu, he would spend the rest of his time doing other chores related to Lakshmi Babu. He would clean his wardrobe, put clothes out in the sun to dry, wipe and clean the floor afresh; sometimes he would shine his dozens of shoes with polish in different colours. Of late, most of the time, he was the one who would also go out to do groceries. Further, on Lakshmi Babu's appeal, he would strive to extend his knowledge from the level that he had already acquired under Lakshmi Babu's guidance in the jail. When he would pick up a book and quietly read it in a corner, the jealousy of the other members of the family surpassed way more than the delight it brought to Lakshmi Babu's face.

Laloo noticed the change in the attitudes of the other servants and members of the family. He felt hurt. He had not yet forgotten his status; he wished to intermingle with the other servants, wanted to keep the master's family happy. But what could he have done? Lakshmi Babu's wish and comfort came before everything else. And he could not foresee a possibility of harmonizing the two extremes that defined his situation.

Nevertheless, he was happy about the fact that he was

successful in always keeping Lakshmi Babu content. As days rolled by, he increasingly became part of Lakshmi Babu's life. Yes, he wasn't only a servant; he was part and parcel of his life. The way Lakshmi Babu was nonchalant about his personal services, Laloo was also similarly relaxed; he felt that his lifeboat was now anchored. He imagined bringing his two sons to Lakshmi Babu's house. With one working and the other studying, his life would be filled with bliss, he thought. In his recent letter to his wife, he had mentioned his plans. How could he deprive his wife of such good news?

Laloo's days passed on in the peace of household routine and comfort until extraordinary circumstances suddenly visited both him and his master.

One day, Lakshmi Babu came back from his evening walk. It was pretty hot. He removed his waistcoat and handed it to Laloo, who hung it in Babu's room. Lakshmi Babu used to keep his fountain pen in his waistcoat pocket. It was a beautiful Parker. Normally, he studied till late at night, a habit he had carried home from his prison days. Of course, in the jail he studied some serious subjects, now he turned the pages of cheap novels sold at railway station book stalls. That night, when everybody had slept, in the middle of his reading he felt the need to note something down and looked for his pen. The pen was not in the pocket. Lakshmi Babu searched for it here, there, everywhere. Laloo might have kept it somewhere, he thought. He was irritated but did not suspect anything. In the morning, he asked Laloo about the Parker. He denied seeing it or keeping it. Lakshmi Babu wondered where the pen had disappeared. Nobody entered his room. Perhaps it fell in the motorcar. The car was searched. Not finding the pen there, Lakshmi Babu concurred that it might have slipped out of his pocket while walking on the river bridge. He could never have doubted Laloo.

A few days later, his golden wristwatch went missing. He came home from work. Before entering the bathroom, he hurriedly removed and left his watch on the table. Laloo had stepped inside the bathroom to put on his clothes and towel. After his bath, Lakshmi Babu got busy with breakfast and other sundry things. Then he dozed off. On waking up, he looked at his wrist. No timepiece. He recalled that he had kept it on the table, but when he looked, the watch was missing. And, upon asking, Laloo again replied not knowing anything about it.

When the pen was stolen Lakshmi Babu did not disclose it to anyone. He went to the market in the evening and bought a similar pen. Nobody knew that his pen had disappeared. He did so lest anyone be unfairly suspicious of Laloo. But hiding the theft of his wristwatch was difficult. The watch, very expensive, was a gift from his in-laws. All along, he had been tying it on his wrist for fifteen years. If not found, people would definitely notice. What should I reply, he thought: 'Should I say I've sent it for repair?' But, why to lie? Self-deception is not virtuous. But then, what happened to the watch? 'I had put it on the table – this I remember very well,' he said to himself as he jogged his memory. Nobody usually enters the room, and no one came in, which is also true. Then, he wondered. He could not show the courage to think further. To digress from his thoughts, he turned over the pages of a book, opened his wardrobe, went to the outhouse and asked the *munshi* about the revenue accounts, after which he went out for an early walk, returned, finished his dinner before time and went to bed earlier than usual.

Despite trying hard, sleep escaped him. He was frequently reminded of the words of the insurance company's director: 'Such people are very slimy, in order to gain trust, they stay decorous, but later they give such a blow that you can only repent'. Has Laloo, too, done the same? Let's put aside the chatter of the insurance company man. These men are motor mouths and garrulous. But, what about that socialist leader? He was pro-poor. He also had said, 'You think that Laloo is happy, but such moments may come when the bundle of currency notes in your purse, your beautiful wristwatch …' Yeah, yeah, in all probability it was such a moment when he …! He could think no further. He tried another perspective. Is it not possible that any other servant might have walked past the same place and taken it. He also considered carrying out a cross-examination of all the servants the following day but realized that such an exercise would lead to a massive hue and cry in the household. Not only inside the home, but outside too. And everyone's suspicion would turn towards Laloo. They would say, this is what one gets for employing a thief. They'd say so, laugh at me and think that I am stupid. I have already suffered monetary loss, why should I be seen as an idiot on top of that? To avoid lying, he decided to travel to his estate the very next day. If people enquired on his return, he would see what to come up with. With this resolution in mind, he also decided to keep an eye on Laloo from then on.

He returned from his estate. When asked, he even replied that the watch was lost. But he diverted the 'when' and 'where' questions. Slowly, his trust began to be restored in Laloo.

Around the same time, like a straw that breaks the camel's back, another incident took place. One day, Lakshmi Babu also found his wallet missing. Lately, he always kept the wallet with him. That day, there were only two ten-rupee notes in it. He firmly believed now that Laloo had turned into a thief again. The socialist leader's view was proven to be true – these rascals are Kaliyugi prophets. But he was actually scared of remembering the proclamation of the insurance company's director. Recollecting his words, Lakshmi Babu was convinced that now Laloo would go for a big hunt and he would be left with nothing else to do but regret. It was now necessary to get rid of him, he thought. Shall I hand him over to the police? These indolent morons deserve no less. Better they rot in the jail. Thinking all this, he was then also reminded of the words of the socialist leader – he had said that Laloo might end up grinding in the same prison. But this was hurled on him as sarcasm, Lakshmi Babu remembered. He resolved that he would also prove to the leader that he was not such a lowly being.

It was evening. Sensing the mood, Laloo himself had a long face and was busy lighting the big table lamp when Lakshmi Babu called him to come close. Without asking anything, Lakshmi Babu put ten currency notes of ten rupees in Laloo's palms. 'Laloo, keep this money and go home now. There is no room for you in my place anymore. My place is not for you anymore. With this money … or …' He couldn't utter another word. 'Babu!' Laloo choked as he tried to speak. 'No, no, go away', said Lakshmi Babu, his face stern. He gestured with his hands for Laloo to leave the room.

After a while, when he was alone, he was humming:

surdas kari kamr par chadhat na dujo rang

(Surdas, no other colour can be put over the black colour).

VI

Laloo had been in a plaintive state since the day Laksmi Babu's fountain pen went missing. Lakshmi Babu did not utter a word about it; on the contrary, to encourage Laloo and keep his spirit high he chattered about random issues and exhibited more love and trust on him. But Laloo had started nurturing a sense of apprehension. He felt as if his good days were over, a crisis was about to unfold. On the exterior, he maintained his earlier demeanour, flaunted the same energy and enthusiasm and tried to smile and appear cheerful in Lakshmi Babu's presence, but an insect had stung deep in his heart, eating into him slowly.

When the watch disappeared, Laloo was convinced that he was done. He also sensed a change in Lakshmi Babu's attitude. The following day, when Lakshmi Babu left for the estate, he figured it out without any delay that he was the reason behind this untimely journey. Further, he observed that Lakshmi Babu's eyes were always on him – eyes that cast suspicion from the front and followed like a detective from the back – that the needle of Laksmi Babu's suspicion pointed to him. Now, despite his conscious efforts, Laloo could not bring back his initial energy and cheer. He remained lost during the day and wept at night. Alas! Those dreams! He was about to bring his two sons, now he felt unsure of his own shelter.

One dreadful night tears kept flowing from Laloo's eyes. He tried to stop them and fall asleep, but to no avail. Before leaving his bed in the morning he decided: 'I'll speak frankly to Babu, fall on his feet, prove my innocence, and, if he fails to believe, I'll beg for his pardon and leave for home. The future is predestined. Many people earn their livelihood in the village, so will I.' As soon as he came across Lakshmi Babu with this resolve, Laloo could not open his mouth or move his hands. As if sensing his mind, Lakshmi Babu assigned him such a task that he would not be free for the entire day. When he went to serve him milk before going to bed, he decided to speak up then. But after taking the glass of milk from his hands, Lakshmi Babu began asking for the well-being of his family in a manner that showed there was not an iota of doubt left in his heart about Laloo's character and actions. Once again, Laloo fell silent – he saw no advantage in scratching an old wound.

And, today, this wallet incident! Lakshmi Babu asked him only once, 'Did you see my wallet?' Hearing the mention of the wallet, Laloo trembled. He felt paralysed. Before he could retrieve his senses, Lakshmi Babu had left. Since then Laloo went into solitude and wept continuously. Lakshmi Babu did not call him for any task, as if he didn't wish to see his face, and when he eventually called, it was to bid him goodbye.

It was dusk already. Lest any other servant or Lakshmi Babu's family members saw him, Laloo left quickly in fear. He was not left with any face to show. He could not even think of his personal belongings and clothes. With long and fast steps, he continued walking. It was noisy outside. The roads were busy. He rammed into people while marching ahead. He had eyes, but they were unable to see; he had ears, but they could not hear. His mind was blank. He was walking out of reflex. Those who he pushed or collided into barked back or scolded him. Once he narrowly escaped coming under an *ekka*, but he did not slow down. He did not even realize this. After he walked some distance away from the crowd, he found himself on a riverbank. In front of him was a bridge where some men were walking. At that moment a beggar-woman appeared out of nowhere and stood in his way. 'Babu! One paisa, please,' she said. Startled, he looked at his hands and realized that the ten-rupee currency notes were still locked in his fingers. He handed all the notes in the old woman's hands. The old woman was astonished. Laloo said, 'Go away, with this money ... or ...!'

With these words, he got up. The darkness of the night was impenetrable now. When he reached the bridge, it was almost deserted. He heard someone play the flute on a distant ghat; its aching sound was audible. He stopped for a moment and looked at the sky – a star was twinkling in the west. Then he looked down into the waters – a fish bounced, making a splash in the water.

'O Mother Ganga, now in only your safe haven ...!'

He jumped over the bridge. A splash again and then the same, usual sound of the waves.

The star in the west was smiling.

Mangar

RAMBRIKSHA BENIPURI

A beefy body. A loincloth wrapped around the waist. A plough on the shoulder. A stick in one hand. A pair of bullocks in the lead. Driving the bullocks while making his rumbling noise, on his way towards my field – since I have been conscious, I believe – I have seen Mangar in the same form.

Yes, I remember, sometimes, in place of the plough, I had the fortune of riding on his shoulders. But such opportunities were very rare because, for reasons unknown, Mangar lacked an innate affection for children, commonly found in men of his kind. Children always ran away from him, and, today, when Mangar is old and fragile, the kids, as if to retaliate, poke him with little sticks and run away. And when he is annoyed, he looks for his walking stick to beat them or hurls abuses at them in irritation. In return, the children burst out laughing and mock him further.

What led to his revulsion towards kids? Isn't it because the only lad that was born to him had betrayed him and passed away much before he could become an earning person? The only daughter he had was lame. And, though he had spent generously at her wedding, once when he had arrived at her doorstep in a time of distress, his son-in-law treated him with such diffidence that Mangar's self-esteem had forced him to flee.

Mangar's self-esteem! Can there be pride in a poor man, too? But that was indeed the inimitable quality of Mangar. He never tolerated anybody's harsh words, and perhaps, in his own mind, he never accorded anyone a status superior to himself. He respected my Baba, possibly due to his old age. I have heard that he liked my father a lot – conceivably, due to his good disposition. But he always considered my uncles as his equal, and, until yesterday, he had been addressing me as 'tu'. Yet how could anyone dare to call Mangar foul-mouthed! Subjection to daily abuse, which was commonly experienced by an average ploughman, was not even a remote possibility in Mangar's case.

Why was it so? There were special reasons: Mangar's burly body was one. More than that, it was his earnest ability to toil to which was added the endearing beauty of his brutal honesty. While others could plough ten *kattha*s in a certain span of time, Mangar managed to do fifteen, and with such unmatchable precision that after the very first round of ploughing, it was difficult to trace any weeds. There was no need to instruct Mangar about which piece of farmland would need ploughing the following day. He surveyed all of them at the end of a workday and, wherever it was required, he reached early in the morning with his plough. There was no need for anyone to monitor

Mangar while he did the tilling. Farmers supervise an average ploughman with sticks and even after that they shirk work, dilly-dally and postpone the work for the next day, but Mangar displayed no such habits. Whether it was to guard the young crops, the dried straw in the field or the crop bundles and food grains in the barn, one could sleep worriless, leaving everything in Mangar's custody.

Where will you find such a labourer? Why won't he be respected and treasured then? My Baba used to say that Mangar was not a ploughman; he was a member of our family. Like a kin sometimes he used to sulk; he also snubbed other members of the family at times. His rebuffs were valued; his sulking was followed by rapprochement.

At times, matters went a little too far. One day there was a heated exchange. The next morning, Mangar did not show up for ploughing, nor did we look for him. If money was not an issue, why won't there be another ploughman available? A new ploughman was hired for tilling the land. In the meanwhile, another farmer brought the news to Mangar: 'Mangaru, look, they have hired a new ploughman. If they have money and can find any number of ploughmen, so do you have your body to find countless householders for work! Come and till the land for us – you will get whatever wage you demand.'

'But what about the fact that I have a headache,' said Mangar. And the headache persisted until my weary uncle went to see him and bring him back. For we realized the value of Mangar in barely four days – the bullocks' shoulders were scratched, their limbs lacerated. The field was tilled, but neither clod nor soil was mixed. Moreover, one had to keep poking the new ploughman throughout the day by sitting in the field's enclosure. After going through so much trouble, barely ten katthas of land were tilled. We soon realized that without Mangar, it was going to be really difficult.

Uncle was standing at Mangar's door. Mangar was sitting inside. Mangar's wife, Bhakolia, said, 'Malik is waiting – go and reconcile with him.' He replied in a loud voice knowing that my uncle was within earshot: 'Tell him I have a headache.' 'Malik, please get his head oiled with Malkin's hair oil,' joked Bhakolia. 'Are you making fun of me?' Mangar's voice was irate. 'Mangar! Come on, mutual misunderstanding is bound to happen at times, excuse us,' said Uncle in a voice that sounded supplicating. Mangar said, 'Please go and get your land tilled by the man who did it for four days – what will you gain from me – you must be saving on rotis, too.' Some arguments, some sulking and rapprochement followed. Then in a while, Mangar, holding the tiller's stick, was walking ahead and behind him was my uncle.

What is this 'saving of roti'? Did you get it? Take it as Mangar's special rent. While every ploughman was offered one roti for his work in the village, it was one and a half for Mangar. The rotis must be fine-grained and well-cooked. There should be a vegetable curry accompanying it because Mangar doesn't take anyone's raw salt. All of Mangar's conditions were met.

But please do not assume that he alone ate one-and-a-half rotis. Did he take a half for his wife? No, he divided that half into two equal parts and fed them to both his bullocks. So, in this way, essentially, the half roti returned to my house, but this way of Mangar's dealing with the allotted rotis was beyond negotiation. Mahadev is hungry and I am eating – how is it possible? For Mangar, these bullocks were not merely bullocks but Lord Mahadev himself.

A couple of times when things went too far, Mangar left my village. But as long as he was in the village, he did not touch the plough for others. He also could not imagine settling down in the other village. Then he looked for a third one, and finally, from the frustration of wandering from one place to the other, came back to my village. Perhaps, he did not find respect anywhere akin to what he had received at my household.

Mangar's nature has always been cold and straightforward. No flattery, no sweet talk. Direct talk, candid dealings. Yet, for some inexplicable reasons, he always looked towards me with affection. Perhaps, because my father endeared him a lot. He still says, 'Manjhle Babu was the true malik; he died, and my kismet was wrecked.' Also, I was an orphan from early childhood. My mother and father had both died. That's why he offered his pious shoulders, and when I grew up a little and started visiting and staying in my maternal village, it was Mangar who often took me there. I used to be on horseback, and Mangar, with the load of my books and gifts on his head, walked ahead holding the reins. On uneven terrain, lest I took a fall, he came by my side and held my body with one hand. Even today I can feel the delicate touch of his strong hands.

As I grew up, my relationship with my home became distant. À la Mangar, I became, a guest in my own house.

But whenever I went home after some gap for a day or two, on two–four months' interval, I saw Mangar in the same profession and demeanour.

Mangar had an aversion to clothes. He always wore a loincloth wrapped around his waist. He did receive dhotis. On the day of Govardhan Puja, would he ever decorate oxen horns without getting a new dhoti? In any case, Baba and uncle gave him old dhotis round the year. On wedding ceremonies in the household, he also received pink dhotis. A kurta was also stitched for Mangar on the occasion of my wedding. But dhotis always ended up becoming his headgear, and a kurta covered his body only if he was visiting our relatives to pass on some message. Normally, he always hung about bare-bodied. And, if I may say, I liked his body the same way. Today I speak from an artist's perspective – Mangar was gifted with a beautiful body.

Jet black – yet beautiful? I don't identify with those who understand beauty as an aggregation of colour and carving, and I am not apologetic for my view even today. Mangar's jet black body was an exquisite specimen of a flawlessly carved human physique. Continuous labour had pumped up his muscles in a natural manner ... unlike wrestlers, whose muscles appear unreal. Every body part – thighs, chest, arms – had ideal shape and size. Neither was there an extra lump of flesh in any part nor was his overall frame like a skeleton. A normal head held atop a perfectly shaped body. The memory of Mangar's body immediately reminds me of the physique of Mr Müller, a proponent of natural exercise. It won't be surprising if that makes a fan of Sandow sad.[1]

As the saying goes – neither does the goddess remain the same, nor does the pagoda. *Aaj na vah devi rahi, na vah kadaah raha.* Mangar is no longer who he used to be. Through his stubbornness, he always kept his poverty covered. But he could not save himself from the assaults of ageing. Each of its beatings continued to tatter him, and today, this idiom seems true for him – *Sukhi haad thaath bhai bhaari, ab kaa ladba he vyapari* (even the bones have become a burden, what else could you carry on the frame of the body).

Not only have the flesh and muscles of his body melted, his bones too have dried out. His body now appears to be a caricature of the old one. Mangar had no savings that could shield him against the assault of old age. *Aaj khaye aur kal ko jhakke, tako gorakh sang na rakkhe!* (Those who worry for the next meal while dining are not allowed in the order of the wandering ascetic) – Mangar, a follower of this proverb, always remained an enemy of the nest egg. No progeny survived to support him in the autumn of his life. From its quiver, age shot this unarmed and unguarded warrior with all its arrows. Mangar was no longer able to furrow the field due to his old age. Initially, he was assigned some odd jobs, but he could not go on for long. Now the only option left for him was to get a pension. But where is the system of pension in this country for ploughmen – the real food suppliers? And the dominion of individual pity has always been petty. Moreover, Mangar perhaps also has the heat and kink of a burnt rope from which the cloud of pity runs away. The cloud of pity needs a gentle stratum of benediction, and Mangar's dictionary always lacked it. On the contrary, even today his language is harsh and dry, and heated with his snub and rebukes, which could vaporize not only water but one's blood as well. Despite such an attitude, sweet drops of liberality drizzled occasionally. They may have quenched a nightingale's thirst; they could not hose the desert of Mangar's dotage. It can be reasonably claimed that we could not have found even Mangar's skeleton had his wife not been there for him.

His other half – Bhakolia. Mangar's ideal partner. *Jamunia* (blackberry) complexion – why should I dishonour her by calling her black-skinned? She had only two kids. That is why she survived the great womanly corrosion, which is given a beautiful epithet of maternity. This is the reason that Bhakolia can move around, while Mangar lies in tatters. She can work and earn a little to sustain two mortals. But for how long? For, even she is petering out day by day.

Bhakolia, Mangar's perfect partner. Not only in physical structure but in character, too. Those were the days when she spoke pointedly, walked hastily. Neither did she let anyone talk back, nor did she tolerate humiliation. Teasing her was like putting one's feet on the hood of a black cobra. But Bhakolia only had the hissing – the allegation of biting and venom will be an injustice to her.

Nonetheless, a woman can remould herself more quickly in the face of changing circumstances than a man, and Bhakolia was an example. Mangar was still the same Mangar – call him rude and crude. But Bhakolia was no longer the same. She babysat for someone, ground spices and thrashed crops for others. She made dung cakes for someone, carried water for others. And whatever she received in return, she served them to Mangar first and then ate herself. Despite doing so much, she had to listen to Mangar's rants and scolding. Mangar emptied all his bitterness and past grudges on her.

Mangar tried forgetting his troubles muttering 'God willing', but the same god made him even more wretched. Last year, he had a severe attack of migraine. Bhakolia, moved by his cry, asked a kind soul for some cinnamons, which she ground and added to goat milk and applied the paste on his forehead. Alleviated from its calming effect, Mangar said, 'Put some on my eyes and brows, too.' Bhakolia followed his orders. But to utter surprise, wherever the paste was applied, a burning sensation erupted. The stinging feeling transformed into a wound, which took away the sight from one of his eyes. When I went home, he said, 'Babuaji, I lost an eye, I am one-eyed now.' After saying this Mangar started crying. Perhaps for the first time, I saw Mangar weep. I was consoling him, but my heart …

And does trouble ever come alone?

Last winter I went home. It was morning. The sun was out. But, as per my old habit, with closed eyes I remained rolled into my quilt. Intermittently, I heard thumping sounds. Removing the quilt from my face, I opened my eyes. Near the heap of straw, I saw a figure almost like a black skeleton trying to stand up, but it kept falling down. What the heck! I got up in surprise and went closer. Oh, it was Mangar! I had heard that Mangar had had a stroke. Seeing him in such a state, my eyes filled with tears. I went to him, held him up and said, 'Why don't you keep lying down, Mangar? It must be hurting.'

'I am bored of lying down, Babua!' Mangar replied. 'Uff!' His veins had slackened, his bloodstream had dried up. Yet, they still had life in them, but his resolve, like the waves of a dried ocean, would wriggle at the sandy shore and retreat beaten. What a tragic scene!

Rama

MAHADEVI VARMA

Neither my siblings nor I can tell when Rama came to our place. In our childhood, just as we were familiar with the assorted contents of Babuji's table, beneath which, in the lull of the noon, inhabited the cosmos of our toys, or knew our huge spring-bed, on which we appeared as heavenly incarnations of turtle and fish when asleep, or the bell and the conch of Ma's *thakurji*, whose offerings we eagerly waited to devour alongside counting the number of bell rings with our eyes half-closed like a heron, in the same way we were eternally acquainted with the short, dark and stout-bodied Rama, from his overgrown toe nails to his long hair.

His white palm, which looked more like a snake's belly, and every single mark on his hands, which had fingers similar to the curvy and knotty tree branches, were all aptly known to us. For we were in perpetual conflict with them, since brushing our teeth in the morning until going to bed at night. It was only during the bedtime stories that a transitory truce was maintained. We knew the soft sound of his dark and heavy feet, which like an old patriarch, holding together his family members, coalesced around the fingers growing in ten different directions. We knew them because they swiftly followed us to our hiding places wherein, after committing mischiefs, we ran to.

Memories of childhood have a mark of uniqueness. When the stream of our emotions is tranquil and stable, then the characters from the past, like the view of things in the fog, progressively become clearer and transparent. But the moment we plan to recall their utility by applying the force of rational argumentation, obliviousness shields them, quite similar to the water moss that momentarily opens up to a falling stone but quickly seals off its view.

Sometimes, Rama's narrow forehead, his extremely thick eyebrows, and tiny affectionate eyes get stamped on my memory board; at other times they slowly turn hazy and disappear completely. The same is true of his ill-carved nose, his widened nostrils caused by incessant airflows, the swollen lips stocking laughter, and a dense, white set of teeth evoking the imagery of yogurt in a black bowl – all were perhaps mistakenly created by an exhausted and irritated sculptor.

Rama's hair had no right to grow even by half an inch. That is why, to give his hair crest a lesson in communism, we walked around with scissors. This crest, however, was like a cat's curling repose. Neither did its master sleep before we went to bed, nor could we dare to do this great act of initiation when he stayed awake.

Perhaps it needs to be admitted now that Rama was ugly, but it was unbearable for us then to even imagine a more splendid companion than him.

In essence, life is the soul of aesthetics, yet it is made tangible through the strokes of harmony than of dissension. As we embroil ourselves with the diversity of exterior forms, we tend to miss the vitality of life that is elemental to those forms. Children are not overtly aware of formalistic diversity; that is why they only recognize life. As soon as they discern life in the beaming ray of love and affection, they straightaway ignore the explicit marks of external differentiation. And if life itself is shielded by the smog of jealousy and hatred, they are not receptive to any of the outward harmony emanating from it either.

This is why we were extremely fond of Rama. It seems he also was not aware of his awful looks. No surprise then that in just a *mirjai* and a knee-long dhoti, which were his regular wear, he exhibited most of his disproportionate body. He didn't, however, lack the required dressing materials. In his room, a long kurta with satin lining, a knotted *safa*, Bundelkhandi shoes and a well-oiled lathi appeared to be waiting for an auspicious occasion. Perhaps, pitying their endless wait and Rama's neglect, our working committee regularly passed the unanimous resolution that by inserting a cane inside the arms of the kurta it should be used as a curtain for our toys, pulling down the basket-like safa from the hanger it could be honoured as a hamper for the dolls and placing the shoes in the water tank the problem of the puppets' river cruise should be resolved permanently. Scolding us, Rama used to lock the bolt of his dark fort's gateways from the top so high that we could not conduct our raid even after climbing on a stool.

The story that we heard of Rama's arrival after growing up was as strange as him. One day, at noon when Ma was drying her inexhaustible *badi-papad* stock in the sun, leaning his head on the gate, a frail and weary Rama was found sitting idle at the courtyard's threshold. Mistaken for a beggar, as soon as she approached him, he fell on her feet saying, 'O Mother, this Rama is dying of hunger.' Nursing him with the linctus of milk and sweets as Ma granted him a second life, the situation became more complicated. For hunger was not such a disease in which medication could be discontinued.

Running away from the tyranny of his stepmother and begging for food all his way through, this rustic child of Bundelkhand reached Indore, where he did not know anybody or have a place to stay. In such a situation, if Rama could easily win Ma's compassion, was it at all so surprising?

That day, when Babuji returned in the evening, he saw Rama's large shoes resting in one corner of the firewood storage and his long cane standing in meditation in the other. And Rama, after his wash up and initiation in the new service, was frantically busy in comprehending the meaning and limit of his duties.

Seeing his odd looks, Babuji was awestruck. He asked Ma laughingly, 'Dharmaraj ji! From which part of the world have you got this creature?' Thanks to Ma, our home was like a zoo. On his return, Babuji often found a lame beggar dining in the outhouse, a blind mendicant playing tambourine and singing devotional songs in the backyard, a poor kid from the neighbourhood in new clothes running around in the courtyard or a poor Brahmin woman packing cereals at the gate of the granary.

Babuji never disapproved any of Ma's activities, but he certainly enjoyed teasing her.

Rama, he thought, was also just another visitor. Not finding any quick answer to Babuji's query about Rama, Ma hastily replied, 'I have employed him as my personal attendant.'

It came as no surprise for a person who hardly rested, despite having any number of servants, a personal helper and, on top of it, such a peculiar character. Babuji almost died laughing and joked affectionately, 'Yeah, I see. Only an attendant moulded in a special frame and capable of terrifying the atheists can stay in service of Dharmaraj (the keeper of dharma)!'

He couldn't trust Rama for his unknown provenance. But it was futile to argue with Ma. For her, the only criterion of judging one's eligibility was her own innate sensibility. Piercing through Rama's horrid looks, her compassion had already scrutinized the simplicity of his heart. To doubt her own judgement about his eternal beauty was impossible for her.

This is how Rama stayed with us, but the problem of ascertaining his duties was not resolved.

For every other chore, there were already enough servants, and Ma could never have handed over the tasks related to worship and kitchen to any of them. Her sacraments and norms regarding rituals of worship were as rigid and archetypal as they were for cookery.

If, on the one hand, she believed that prayer and contemplation were required for her soul, on the other, she also firmly held the belief that doing her own cooking was absolutely necessary for our bodies.

All of us siblings were only a couple of years younger or older to each other, so there was not much lag in our respective transitions from innocence to maturity. Like demons are continuously busy with disrupting *yajna*, we roved around looking for opportunities to obstruct Ma's every mission. Thus, by bestowing upon Rama the uphill task of taming us rebels, Ma could be at peace now.

Early in the morning, Rama cleaned the prayer room and rinsed bright its utensils with lemon. Then he came to wake us up. No one knew how many turns and twirls had occurred in our sleeping positions on that colossal bed by the morning. Someone's legs were found entangled with the other's neck; one's entire body was weighed over another's hand; somebody's back walled someone else's breath. To take stock of every possible situation, Rama's hard hands, which remained disguised behind their soft touch, travelled from one corner of the quilt to the other. Then he carried us along, on foot or on his shoulders, to the daily ceremonies of brushing and washing up.

Our wash up was not at all an easy ceremony. Rama had to continuously chant the great coronation mantra: *Doodh batasa raja khaye*, 'A raja eats sweet and milk'. But, we were not ready to accept each other's coronation. When

Rama used to call me 'Raja', Nanhe Babu (the little master) would open his sparrow-like mouth and tweet, 'Lama, why do you call her laja?' The pride of this tiny man, who was even unable to pronounce 'r', made me upset, perhaps. While the *chakravyuh* of Rama's left-hand fingers closely encircled my head, his *sudarashan-chakra*-like right palm, marked with three dark lines, groped my face in search of grime. In spite of bearing so much pain, accepting others' crowning was tantamount to announcing one's failure. So, deploying all fair and foul means, I compelled Rama to address only me as 'Raja'. Rama knew the ultimate mantra to indulge such combatants. He whispered in my ears, 'You are the greatest of kings, O little baby.' Perhaps he said exactly the same into the ears of the little master because he would joyously put his tiny fingers in the jar of tooth powder and begin to rub his lips instead of his teeth. Rama was deeply averse to such acts, so I looked down upon him with pride, as if he was a stupid soldier disobeying the orders of his commander.

Afterwards, we three deities were installed in a queue and Rama came with small and big spoons, a bowl of milk and a plate of fruits to please such strange divinities who were belligerent to prove one's superiority over the others. But he was a seasoned devotee. By what force of devotion he managed to get these idols to eagerly partake the offerings made by a crow, no one knew. As soon as we closed our eyes, there reached a grape in the mouth, a biscuit beneath the teeth or a spoon full of milk in between the lips. We only pretended not to see because all of us saw the performance of Rama's dark and thick juggling fingers with eyes half open. And, in fact, I was scared of the black, hard and unknown beak of the crow. Had I not identified Rama's fingers and hands in the imagined crow and its mandible, I would have certainly run away from the allure of the offerings.

Rama's assiduous task did not end with the completion of the breakfast rites. Protecting our eyes from the surfs of soap and not letting our earlobes become dry islands during bath, maintaining the caste-like irrational discrimination between the wrong and the right side of the cloth while dressing us, judging the balance between the quantity of food and the recipient's limit while feeding us, eliminating the scarcity of an elephant, a horse, or a flying carriage in the course of playing and carrying us to the threshold of a dream world with his arms spread like feathers over us through his marvellous storytelling were all Rama's duties.

As unfathomable was Rama's affection for us, so was our limitless cruelty towards him. One day, upon our insistence to visit the Dussehra fair and, consequently, after persistent appeals from Rama, Ma finally granted him permission to take us to the fair grounds. To buy toys, he put one sibling on his shoulders and took another in his lap. Then asking me to hold his finger, he advised, 'O Raja Bhaiya, don't you forsake the finger.' Granting my agreement to his instruction with a nod, I anyway at once had decided to roam in the fair alone. After wandering around and saving myself from getting trampled, when I felt hungry I naturally remembered Rama. Stopping at a sweetmeat shop, hiding my anxiety I asked, 'Have you seen Rama? He has been lost.' Spilling parental affection from his misty eyes, the old sweet-maker asked, 'What does your Rama look like?' Pressing my lips together, I replied with confidence, 'He is very good.' How difficult it must have been to identify Rama with such a description! Thinking of the same difficulty perhaps the old man requested me to take rest at his shop for a while. I didn't want to accept my defeat, but my legs were tired and the plates decorated with sweets were no less inviting. So, sitting on a rug in a corner like a guest, I accepted the old man's offerings in the form of sweets and began to tell the tale of my great journey.

In search of me, on the other hand, Rama was almost dying. Finally, by the evening, upon enquiring everyone on his way, when Rama reached the shop after much difficulty, I asked him with pride, 'Despite being such a grown-up man, you lost your way, Rama?' On his parched face rolled tears of joy as dewdrops on dried petals. Moving me this way and that, he ensured that it was me who was standing in front of him. He inspected me as if I had lost a part of my body in the fair. After returning home, I realized that such adventurous acts of pride, in the dictionary of adults, is considered as crime. However, taking my delinquency on his head, it was Rama who bore all the scolding. And yet it was me who was the special recipient of Rama's tender patting when he took all of us to bed.

Once, trying to teach us the minute and profound difference between the objects belonging to oneself and to others, Rama decided to become a clever commentator. And then, what more was required! His lecturing was enough to activate our grey cells into scheming – whose objects could be grabbed and brought over so as to watch Rama's small eyes fill with disappointment and helplessness.

Our house was so closely aligned with a Thakur Saheb's building that it was possible to ferry from one rooftop to the other, but the pathway was a half-feet narrow wall and a fall from there could have facilitated a survey of the netherworld.

After ascertaining that the flowers in the courtyard of that house could come under the definition of someone else's object, we took the aerial route one day to steal them with the sole intention of teasing Rama. Had anyone's foot slipped, the story would have been different, but fortunately we landed safely on the adjoining rooftop. On the last step of the staircase leading towards the ground floor, a bitch had settled with her little puppies, and at their sight itself, we changed our decision on the object of burglary. As soon as we lifted one of the puppies, the helpless mother began a fearsome barking of protest. When the housemaster came out of the drawing room and the slothful mistress also rushed out of the bedroom, we were faced with an insurmountable dilemma. What to do in such a situation was not at all part of Rama's lessons, so we disclosed our intentions on the basis of our own intelligence: 'We came through the roof to steal flowers.' The housemaster broke into laughter and asked, 'Then why don't you steal them?' He received a more earnest response than he expected, 'We will steal a puppy now.' By the time we returned with the puppy via the legitimate route, Rama had come to know about our robbery. Witnessing poisonous fruits growing on the elixir tree of his sermons, he must have been deeply perturbed. Lifting the chief of the robbers by her ear, he asked, 'Where have you been to?' I used to find whining quite insulting, so I bore the punishment by clenching my teeth. Later, with controlled rage, I complained to Ma, 'By pulling my ears extremely hard, Rama has twisted and elongated them. Please call the doctor to fix them and lock up Rama in the dark room.' As she was ignorant of our crime and Rama could not have divulged our secret in this lifespan, he had to listen to a long lecture on the psychology of mistreatment of children. He was truly ashamed of his behaviour, but the more he tried to persuade his Raja Bhaiya, the more she recalled her earache. However, seeing him sitting distraught outside that evening, I proposed a truce by saying, 'Sing a song for me.' Rama knew only one devotional song, '*aiso siya raghubir bharose*' (so was Sita counting on lord Rama), and the manner in which he sang could have chased away a crow or, for that matter, any bird resting on the trees. But we were incredible listeners of an inimitable singer – Rama sang only for us and we only listened because it was him.

My childhood was a little different from that of the contemporary girls' and that is why Rama has a special place and significance in it.

Those days, girls were not welcome in a family. From itinerant female singers in the courtyard, the drummers and family elders to young boys at the veranda, all of them sat waiting for a son. As soon as the news of a Lakshmi's arrival was whispered, an appalling gloom spread over in every nook and corner of the house. An old woman would signal the silent singers to leave and the elderly men would gesture the quiet musicians to depart. As it was beyond the capacity of a family to bear the burden of such a guest, so the means to unceremoniously dispatch her were also not infrequently observed.

Whether such a thing ever happened in our family, I don't know. But when no goddess visited for long, people in the house started getting worried. As it was impossible to perform the royal rite of *ashwamedha* without a horse, it was impossible to perform the great rite of *kanyadan* without a daughter.

When I was born after a long interlude, my grandfather received me as a special blessing of his family deity Durga. In order to show respect to the divinity, and, in that moment, keeping aside all his knowledge of Persian, he found such a magnificent mythological name that nobody dared to counter its grandeur by giving me any other lighter appellation. It is futile to mention that to make me compatible with this name, everyone started filling me with so much knowledge and wisdom from my childhood that my tender head turned rebellious. Whether I could have ever become familiar with the simplicity of life without an illiterate Rama's affectionate shadow, I am really doubtful. My initiation into slate-writing was over. By pointing fingers at any one letter of the alphabet, I could now invoke a variety of words beginning with the same letter and express a range of feelings. Among my siblings I was, therefore, no less significant than the legendary Shukracharya, the guru of demons. I had acquired the ability to find approval and disapproval of any of their actions in my book. For this, they had to remain ever vigilant. No sooner had the little brother (Nanhe Babu) jumped, than I opened the book and read, 'A monkey comes to show his dance.'[1] As soon as my sister sulked, I recounted, 'Why to appease a sulking girl, she will come around on her own.'[2] My siblings were extremely apprehensive of my scriptural knowledge because they did not have the resources to similarly exemplify my acts. But the literate Shukracharya was often defeated by the illiterate Rama. Rama had such an encyclopaedic collection of proverbs, legends and tales that they exceeded hundreds of such books. As a result, whenever my scriptural knowledge caused a great Indian war, taking over the position of a judge he would whisper his rulings in everyone's ears and broker peace.

Rama had no objection to Panditji, the Hindi teacher. In the middle of my playtime when emerged Maulavi Saheb – the Urdu teacher, music teacher and drawing master, Rama's heart was filled with resentment. Perhaps he knew that I would not be able to bear so much of the burden of accomplishment.

I became so scared of Maulavi Saheb that one day, to excuse myself from his lessons, I had to hide inside a big basket. Unfortunately, it was the same basket in which some leftover mangoes sent by Grandpa were lying. In order to empty and refill the basket with something else when Rama, perplexed over its weight, carried it to Ma, the situation turned really serious. As he removed the cover, I could see no option but to run away. Eventually, with the combined efforts of Ma and Rama, I was freed from taking Urdu lessons.

I had no complaints of my drawing master, for he didn't stop me from playing. On every sheet, by drawing two vertical straight lines and placing a circle on top, I portrayed Rama. When I had to sketch someone else, a few more random pencil strokes were added into the same frame.

However, neither I nor Rama was happy with Narayan Maharaj. On the very first day when he enquired about my knowledge of music, I confidently answered that I learn from Rama. On his request to sing, I sang the same devotional song that Rama sings and he was speechless. In spite of this, when he refused to acknowledge my devotee-teacher Rama as more superior and eligible than himself, it was natural for me to be unhappy with him.

That the world could have functioned without Rama, we were not ready to accept. Whenever Ma left to see Naani for ten-fifteen days, Rama had to stay back to look after Babuji and the house. Without Rama, we were never convinced of leaving, hence Ma felt compelled to leave us behind, too.

In times of sickness, it was difficult to find a more dedicated and careful attendant than Rama. Once, when my younger brother had smallpox, Rama stayed with him quarantined on the top-floor room in such a manner that we did not remember our brother. Because of his attentiveness, I was never infected with smallpox.

Once more, because of him, I escaped an extremely dangerous disease. Indore was invaded by the plague, and we were staying on the outskirts of the city. Ma and my brother, who was only a couple of months old, were so ill that Babuji hardly got time to care for the remaining three of us. On such occasions Rama enfolded us with his love in such a way that it was impossible to feel any kind of dearth.

Sitting on a see-saw hanging from the trunk of a mango tree, we often listened to Rama's fantastic stories. On one of these days, a tumour appeared beneath my ear and gave me a light fever. Rama had narrated a tale of an old woman from whose swollen leg, with god's grace, a mighty frog was born. Giving this news to Rama, I said, 'It seems that the same legendary frog will come out of my ears.' He was stunned. Wrapping warmed pebbles in a wet cloth, it is difficult to recount how many times he fomented the lump with this padding. What he murmured while applying the warm pack I didn't understand; I could only discern a few names of goddesses, gods and Lord Hanuman. He didn't leave my bedside for two days and two nights. On the third day my swelling levelled, but Rama was infected with a very high fever. A cyst had developed which was operated upon and he remained seriously ill. After a while, when Ma could take us to the bed of frail Rama, a faint smile ran over his dried lips. An enthusiasm appeared in his sunken eyes and a string of energy ran through his weak body. Ma said, 'Rama, you had saved her. If we were not able to save you, we would have repented all our lives.' In his answer, moving his hand which had overgrown nails, Rama touched Ma's feet and wiped his eyes. After Rama recovered Ma often told him, 'Rama, now you should set up your own household so as to enjoy the pleasures of paternity.' 'O Bai what do you say! What would I do with my own worthless children! May my Raja stay blessed, she will take good care of her Rama,' he always replied. He talked so much about his imagined children that not only did we assume them to be real but also identified them as our rivals. We were sure if his children were like us, he would not have talked about them with such epithets as hopeless creatures, rascal, etc.

One day, when he came out of his room into the courtyard with his lathi, shoes and the pink safa on his head, we all grew extremely apprehensive, for we had never seen him dressed so well. Looking suspiciously at his cane, I couldn't resist asking, 'Rama, are you going to beat those children?' Waving his stick in the air, he replied laughing, 'Yes, Raja Bhaiya, I'll hit those losers so hard that …' But Rama left and God knows for how long we had to make new plans every day to avoid the tough hands of Kallu's mother.

For us, after an eternity, but for others after some time, one day, dressed in a saffron safa and pink dhoti, Rama appeared at the gate in the morning and began shouting, 'Raja Bhaiya! Raja Bhaiya!' We all ran out clumsily but stopped in dismay on the veranda. Rama was not alone. A veiled woman, who was standing behind him in a red sari wearing bangles and anklets around her wrists and legs, made us simultaneously curious and suspicious.

When Munni, my younger sister began swinging holding on to Rama's kurta, the pair of piercing eyes from under the nose-length veil opposed her act. As Nanhe Babu insisted to ride on Rama's shoulders, a prohibitive vibration was discerned in the head hiding inside the veil. Crouching down when I tried to look up to that novel face, the idol turned around. How could we have been pleased with such a visitor? Gradually, as the days passed by, the seeds of a great Indian war began to sprout in Rama's dark room, and the possibility of famine in our playful universe was heightened. For building the city of our toys, Rama was a divine architect as well as a demonic destroyer, but now he didn't get recess to perform his epic duty. No sooner would he come to us than the veiled idol would also appear following him. And due to her silent non-cooperation, it was not only us but also our dollies that felt suffocated. To address this, our war committee met. A king should sit on an elevated place, so I positioned myself on a table from where my feet couldn't touch the ground. The honourable minister occupied a chair and the army-chief sat on a stool. Then the raja spoke somberly, 'Why has Rama brought her?' The minister also nodded and repeated, 'Why has Rama brought her?' And, to hide his inability to pronounce 'r', the army chief spoke while rotating his eyeballs up and down, 'True, why has he brought her?'

Then that unique committee unanimously decided that the creature who has arrived to violate the domain of our sovereign rights must be punished for protecting the dignity of justice. As per the law, this task was assigned to the army chief.

When Rama's wife prepared chapatis, the little master stealthily dropped biscuits in the kitchen; when she went to shower, he pulled down her clean sari from the hanger. God knows how many such punishments were meted out to her, but from her side, neither a plea for forgiveness nor the proposal of truce was made. In fact, she became firmer in her resistance and began to take revenge of our mistreatment from Rama. An impenetrable knot of harshness always marked her dark face and the shadow of anger did not alight from her black eyeballs. So, like us, the innocent Rama was clueless in the beginning, then upset and finally became rebellious. Perhaps, he could not resolve how to submit his entire time and fondness at his wife's feet, and if he did so, how would he survive? And then one day, in anger Rama's wife left for her home.

Rama, it so appeared, felt liberated from the unpleasant bond. By getting rid of his wife he again became the happy creator of our unique universe, as if her presence was merely a line drawn with water.

But Ma was intolerant of any form of injustice. That Rama had thrown his wife, out like our old toys, she felt, was extremely unfair. So, Rama began receiving long and complex lectures on righteous conduct and the duties that come with responsibility. Rama's departure seemed to have the same commiserative compulsion as that of a student who, because of his father's love, is going to endure the teacher's beating.

His return could not be possible after that parting. After a long time it was heard that he had fallen ill at home. Ma sent money and wrote a letter calling him back but, on the pathways of life, he was no longer destined to walk with us any further.

With toys arranged, we kept looking for him in the vacuum. Nanhe Babu wanted to travel across seven seas, but his journey was to be suspended due to non-availability of the flying horse. Munni was desperate to tour the world by boarding her train, but it was not possible to run and halt the train without the man showing green and red flags. I had to arrange for the wedding of my doll, but in the absence of the priest and the manager, the auspicious occasion was being perpetually postponed.

My youngest brother, who increased our count to four was now two and a half years old, was successfully busy practising the skill of turning our creations into ruins. Placing him in the middle of our toys, we, one by one, narrated Rama's story and then informed him that he would not be able to carry out any mischief after Rama returned in his pink safa and holding his lathi. But Rama didn't bother to return even for the conclusion of our story.

I am so old now that the insistence to be called 'Raja Bhaiya' appears like a dream; the legends and tales of childhood seem fanciful, and the splendid world of toys is now a delusion. But even today Rama is true, beautiful and memorable. Standing tall on my past, Rama's towering shadow continues to grow in the present – silently, tirelessly, but affectionately.

Sabia

MAHADEVI VARMA

Sabia is neither an abbreviation of Shabnam nor of Shabrat. It is a vernacular derivative of the classical Savitri. If truth be spoken, either our Aryan magnanimity allowed the lowest among the Harijans to be purified in the shadow of this proper noun or, deceiving everyone's eyes like a clever pickpocket, Sabia's parents, ideally resting in heaven but ipso facto in hell, picked this treasured name. And, to make it their own, they chiselled it so well that now it has become difficult to prove anyone's exclusive claim on this word.

As if to oppose my principle of not firing a servant, when the old *jamadar* left without my permission for his final journey – from where no one could be brought back – at that point in time appeared Sabia, carrying a month-old baby who looked more like a lump of flesh,[1] draped in tattered clothes and holding the fingers of her five-year-old Bachiya, whose nudity was covered with dirt. Her face appeared moulded in shiny black clay, but each of the lines on Sabia's face had the same perfection of appearance as is often seen in the sculptures designed from plaster of Paris. Because the shape of her eyes was not elongated but round, they had a consternating look akin to a child lost in a fair. Heavy and lustreless steel bangles around her ankles and wrists gave her the look of a prisoner. On her narrow forehead the beauty of a yellow glass bindi, glued atop her connected eyebrows, invoking the memory of a midden adorned with wild eggplant flower.

Draped in a dhoti, which was once red but now resembled the colour of an old earthen pot, Sabia appeared like a terracotta figurine moulded painstakingly by a naïve sculptor. The figurine's colour was washed out and now only its clay, neatly fastened with the well carved lines, was peeping irregularly from all over.

I came to know that her husband had left for *pardesh* without informing her. She was in childbed then and fell ill in grief. In the bungalow where she worked as a servant, arrived another *mehtarani* and replaced her. If she finds some work here, her children would be reared.

Ignoring her promise of working with dedication, I looked suspiciously at the little bale and asked, 'How will you work carrying it?' Nodding confidently and stroking the soiled and skinny back of her daughter when Sabia elucidated the little girl's extraordinary skills in looking after her brother, I could neither laugh nor resist smiling.

Indeed, watching a gloomy seriousness spread on her firefly-like eyes, it was cruel to laugh at the little girl, and yet insensitive to remain nonchalant.

When, after instructing Sabia about the work, I came

inside the room from the veranda, old Bhaktin's curiosity broke bounds of my fear and inundated Sabia with her innumerable questions. A tireless tale teller that she was, the topmost principle of Bhaktin's life was to know everything about everybody. And it seems, by the grace of Almighty the great storyteller himself, she was blessed with a mile-long tongue to achieve this task. The snippets of her questionnaire – dispersed as they were like the thousand-beads of her rosary – forcibly entered my ears. My inability to avoid them, perhaps, lay in the compassionate answers.

I could not clearly hear the questions regarding Sabia's husband, but the tone of her answer – 'No mother, there was no fuss, my husband was a nice man' – indicated that the speaker's voice was choking. In reply to 'that woman was really strange!', Sabia clarified in a drained voice, 'Mother, to each according to her destiny.' Then I made a conscious effort to concentrate on writing and the thread of the conversation was dropped there. Gradually, I got to know that Sabia's husband is not a derivative of Satyavan. Not only that, he was meaningless as his name, Maiku. One day he left with a clansman's new wife, only God knows for where. And, that too, at a time when Sabia was indisposed with a half-a-week-old infant. Neither did Sabia quit her hope for his return, nor had news about him arrived since. The proposal to remarry which this poor clansman put before Sabia, partly to take revenge and partly to restore his withered home, was nevertheless met with rejection. Finally, following *once bitten twice shy*, he anointed an elderly widowed sister-in-law as the goddess of his home and breathed in solace. If, consequently, everyone began to call Sabia eccentric, what was surprising about it? But, save her passion for work, I did not find any trace of eccentricity in her. Right in the morning, she would spread a tattered and soiled piece of cloth on the pebbled ground under the neem tree and lay her baby on it. And then, leaving his sister beside him, somewhat for protection as also to fan away the flies, she would fasten her threadbare mantilla on her waist before getting ready with the broom. Along with the scraping tune of her broom, then, began the dance of flying Sabia in one corner of the compound, in another corner commenced the performance of the metaphor called Bachiya. Changing her postures from *virasan* to *yogasan*, now she chased away the flies with her tiny hands, then she drove away the crows by jumping on her one or two little feet. Instead of the stiffness of a dry stick, the mother's lean body was springy like a green twig, which symbolized life rather than frailty. As opposed to the bopping of a tender leaf, the girl's skeletal body swayed like a wilted bud, which signified stasis, not growth. The neem tree, opposite my window, was the young girl's stage; important spectators, such as my puppy and the hostel's kitten were anyway most welcomed there. Even the alien crows, unnamed birds and a familiar squirrel, the neighbour who stayed on the same neem tree, were also no less entertained. Looking at Bachiya's plain attentiveness, it nevertheless appeared that every being, from the puppy and the birds to the squirrel and the flies, were desperate to grab and run away with her darling brother. Perhaps, to make these masquerading raiders pliant, she spoke in countless languages – from a cat's meow to a bird's chirp, and, in the end, like a trumpet of truce, she played a pipe that was bought for a penny.

Tearing the ramparts of her dutifulness when hunger rankled deep inside her, she would begin to make a compromise with this hidden enemy by taking out a loaf of bread that had been kept folded in a corner of the same soiled cloth. But it should be conceded that this task of unfolding and eating the bread became unimaginably arduous in the presence of so many eager spectators. Once, as she began to complain in the voice of a rooster, a rebel raven snatched away her only weapon to fight hunger. Finally, by sending a biscuit and a laddoo, it felt that I had accomplished the holy task of replacing her wooden dagger with a machine-gun. Since then, Bachiya's request regularly reached me via 'cock-doodle-doo', and in reply what I used to send was always embossed with Bhaktin's taunt.

After finishing her work by ten o'clock, Sabia would gather her creations like a juggler and go for a wash. By the time she returned with a well-rinsed and shining brass plate to collect food, the long-drawn bustle in the hostel related to lunch used to be over. 'The leftovers were not meant to be thrust onto the jamadar, but should be fed to the bullocks of the school's cart' – due to this strict and unconventional instruction from me, in addition to the fresh dal and rice that Sabia received from the kitchen, what kind of bitter sarcasm she might have regularly received from the *maharajin* and the *kaharin*, I can only imagine. Sabia was so hesitant to complain about anyone, as if the mere usage of complaining words would cause ulcer in her mouth.

Seeing kid-laden Sabia barely managing to carry the plate, I suggested that she feed herself and her children in the hostel. She replied with such shame as if it was an acceptance of an unpardonable crime. She said, 'Malkin, Bachiya has a blind grandmother. How will we eat without feeding her first?' Telling her anything was meaningless, but I was infuriated with Maiku who had left the burden of his blind mother along with two children upon the aggrieved and frail Sabia. A man is really a strange creature. He is capable of inflicting severe pain on the woman for the tiniest of his pleasures, and he does so with such assurance as if this is what she deserves. He wants all his responsibilities coated in sugar, like quinine pills. At the first whiff of bitterness, he runs away, leaving all concerns behind.

I developed a mindful affection for Sabia's effortless decency, and her days were passing by well.

Suddenly, one day, Bhaktin, acting as an interpreter for Sabia who was hiding behind the door, said that she needed a good sari. I granted my permission to give the khadi sari that was drying on the rope-hanger. But pulling a disproving face, Bhaktin said, 'Better than that.' Then I got up and began the search for saris which could fall into the category of this indeterminate adjective.

My hands reached a blue silk sari that had faded due to incessant washing; it belonged to the time when I had not yet quit wearing silk. Throwing the same sari before Bhaktin, I went back to my work. I never have the desire to know more than anyone is willing to share on her own, so I didn't ask anything about this untimely request for a sari. But Bhaktin could not survive without supplementing this deficiency of my character. Not only for others, she is also an object of curiosity for me as well. No matter how important a task I may be doing, she would sit within my earshot and loudly recite countless stories to herself, of course, with the intention of making me hear them. I have scolded her a number of times, but there has been no change in her nature. Since she came to me leaving behind an orchard with eighteen mango and five mahua trees, twenty-five *bigha*s of agricultural land and breaking up with three daughters, their husbands and many grandchildren, the possibility of quitting and going back to her village has not entered her mind. She is not willing to leave even if I do not give her wages. She is ready to bring her own food – *gur* and *sattu* – from the village and live here, even if I don't give her anything to eat. She will only go to heaven after leaving me, that too not by her wish. Is it possible to reform such a person? This is how she continuously plays the role of Sanjay. The only difference is that in the Mahabharata Sanjay supplied the news from the warfront and pleased the eyes of the blind Dhritrashtra only when asked, but to her myriad unsolicited stories, I have to often bear the grief of turning deaf.

Oh yes! So, I came to know from Bhaktin that Maiku came back, but with Genda. He, however, made her a guest in the house of a jamadar employed at the railway station. Poor Sabia went mad with happiness and that very day arranged for the recital of *Satyanarayan Katha*. When things settled down, Maiku sat with a long face. Upon asking a number of times, he talked about Genda and pleaded with Sabia to go and get her home. Not only that, looking at Sabia's silk sari, he begged her, 'It doesn't go well on your dark skin, Sabia. Give it to Genda, it will look amazing on her.'

Without uttering a single word, Sabia removed the blue sari and put it in Maiku's hands. Wearing an old sari, despite her blind mother-in-law's remonstrations, she went to bring Genda home. But obviously, it appears, that her heart was broken. She often cries, leaning her head on the neem tree and, at times, pauses to wipe her eyes while dusting. Oh, poor Sabia! For long, she waited for him, keeping him intact in her memory. Now that he has returned, he is with Genda, and what is more, he has neither enquired about Sabia's plight nor has he looked towards his children once. Believing Genda's fake complaints, he only fights with Sabia. Sabia's burden has further increased because Maiku has not found any job yet.

One day, Sabia brought the wheatish-complexioned, round-faced, wicked and chirpy Genda wearing the same blue sari and said, 'Malkin, the younger sister conveys her regards to you!' Wonderful – what blessing could I have given? Saying 'stay blessed' would have meant, keep giving pain to Sabia. So I said, 'May god give you wisdom to live harmoniously.'

Four or five days later Sabia came again. She wanted five months' salary, that is, ₹50, calculating ₹10 a month, in advance. I asked in surprise the reason for such a request. Then I came to know that Genda's first husband and his caste-members were creating troubles. The poor elderly caste-men needed to be treated with a feast so that they could get the strength to tolerate this Mahabharata-like great quarrel. Not rewarding the ex-husband for his unqualified well-mannerism would have tantamounted to ignoring the principle of self-sacrifice! Even for such an important cause, I did not wish to starve Sabia's children to death; I had to give some money. When I heard that Sabia sold a *hamel*, the last souvenir of her late mother, to arrange for the remaining money, I regretted. I must have known that this woman, once she made a commitment, did not know how to step back.

In spite of the unanimous acceptance of Genda's stay in that home, Sabia's difficulty did not lessen as she relentlessly fought with Sabia. Yet, on seeing Sabia carrying a jug of daal and a plate full of rotis and rice twice a day, my mind was astonished. Despite receiving embers for herself, her canopy of affection was still capable of bestowing a tranquil shadow upon others. Just as she did not mind the mischiefs of her innocent children, she ignored the heartless betrayal of her husband, unfair sarcasm of the co-wife, and the uncalled-for denunciation of her mother-in-law. It was as if everyone was a child before her, so their failings did not make her forgo her duties. In response to criticism for Maiku's behaviour, she had a simple and precise counter-question – had he gone mad or were suffering from a dreaded disease, what advice would people have given her? No matter how irrational her answer was, it does clearly explain Sabia's heart. She is not one of those women who can supplement the lightness of her husband's character with the weight of his bungalow, car, property and so forth. Neither can she be counted among those dwelling in the 'torture-chamber' guarded by an alert and heartless religion. Nor could she be one of those on whose blemished head hangs the naked sword of society. She will be called the lowliest being on all counts. Then how could one explain the existence of this touchstone of purity, who could turn even a piece of iron into gold?

In all these years only once have I noticed Sabia disappointed. Maiku and Genda had not returned after visiting a village fair. The same time a theft took place in a nearby bungalow. Upon such occurrences, who doesn't know how rich men, who themselves have turned wealthy by robbing others, not only hand over their own servants but also poverty-stricken poor strangers to the canines. No matter whether they retrieve even a penny or not, in their sadist anger they don't stop short of stripping the unfortunates of their scarce dignity. Terrified of the possibility of arrest, Sabia muttered, 'My husband will not be spared', and began crying before me. Her grief touched my heart in an unprecedented way and left me astounded. Values that a society has fixed for a woman's conduct are not the only measure of her greatness. The limits of dignity and conduct that a woman herself etches out in her soul is far deeper and firmer than those of the norms specified by society. It is because of this that even in the heart of a woman, who trades off her life as per the demands of the social system, purity can remain intact; and alternatively, a virtuous woman leading the life as per the regulations and restrictions of religion and society can continue to remain involved in the continuous practice of vileness. Eventually, the new trouble that had dawned upon Sabia dissipated. How it happened, however, is not related to her story.

Pointing at the same virtuous and dutiful Sabia, when a barrister's wife asked, 'Why do you hire a thief's wife as a servant?', my icy anger became as razor-sharp as the water that could slice with its thin edge not only the mud but the boulders, too. Unintentionally, I blurted, 'If making other's wealth one's own by hook or crook is theft, then who amongst us rich does not qualify to be called a thief's wife?' Noticing the darkness that spread across the face of the questioner, I was not less aggrieved either, but the arrow had not only left the quiver but had also pierced its target.

The truth is that I find Sabia closer to the legendary womanhood of the mythological Savitri who extended the frontier of life to the unknown realm. If the latter had to fight with death for the sake of life, the former has been struggling with life to avoid being dead.

Ratnaprabha

JAINENDRA KUMAR

Townspeople queue up to take a dip in the Yamuna since the crack of dawn. Of them, women come in greater numbers. From the last hours of the night until late morning, women of different types, kinds and ages can be seen marching afoot, alone, in groups, in all sorts of carriages covering the distance between Chandni Chowk and Yamuna Ghat. This always makes for a splendid sight to behold.

For the past month or so, a big new car visits the Yamuna at a scheduled time. Everybody knows that the car belongs to a *sethani*. A famous merchant, Lakshminivasji, has been newly married the third time. In marriage he has received an extremely worthy, learned and beautiful wife. Her name is Ratnaprabha; it is she who visits the ghat in the car regularly. Passers-by or bystanders at the ghat stare at her and the car, awestruck. All feel bewildered at her confident demeanour. She doesn't keep a veil. Her beauty is flawlessly attractive. The purity of modesty is reflected in her behaviour; ornaments are hardly visible on her body. A mere set of bangles that are thinner than a straight line are the only jewels that adorn her wrists. She always wears milky-white and clean clothes. She routinely brings two baskets of flowers to the Yamuna. One she bestows upon the river, another upon god. She doesn't bathe in the Yamuna, though; she anoints its water in her eyes and on her forehead, then sprinkling it atop herself, she bows to the mother Yamuna before sitting in a designated corner for a *jaap*. After the deity *darshan*, she leaves. The surroundings, it so feels, brims over with grace and the aristocratic bearing of her persona.

One day she spotted a young man with a *ramnami* dupatta fastened to his waist, singing along and selling books. He is to be found at the same place and time doing exactly the same thing on most days. The upper part of his body is uncovered. He must be twenty or twenty-two years old. He is dark-complexioned and has an attractive build. His hair flows long and curly. A beard has begun to emerge.

The sethani observed all this while the car slowly made its way through the crowds. She also noticed that the bookseller would look up at the car when it drove past him.

Ratnaprabha is accustomed to having people gawk at her. Yet, without directly observing, she had noticed that the youth's gaze towards her and the car were of the same nature, as if she were also an object.

Ratnaprabha even looked back at him a couple of times. But unlike others he did not lower his eyes. His eyes didn't lower out of respect as it often happened with others. The young man kept staring in the same manner.

This happened near the ghat. The vehicles there move slowly due to the crowds and the narrowness of the road. As the car pulled over suddenly, she said to the chauffeur, 'This guy who sells books, call him over.' When called, the youth came and stood before her. He had books in his hand. From inside the car, Ratnaprabha asked, 'What's that?'

'Books. Do you want any?'

Ratnaprabha said, 'It's not about books. Why don't you do your work properly?'

The young man couldn't comprehend the import of her sentence and remained standing still.

'You better keep your eyes down. Listen! Go away! …' 'You drive the car,' she said to her driver.

The car went away and the youngster remained unmoved. Then, he also went back to his usual spot.

However, she observed that his gaze involuntarily followed the moving car. He kept staring after it, his eyes filled with surprise.

After a couple of days, Ratnaprabha called him once again and asked, 'What do you sell?'

'Books. *Hanuman Chalisa*, *Stri-Subodhini*, *Tota-Maina*, *Chabili-Bhatiyari* – do you want any?'

Ratnaprabha felt very bad. She said, 'Why do you sell these obscene books?[1]'

'It sells so I sell. I also have THAT one … Do you want?'

'What?'

The chap whispered, '*Kokshastra*?'

Ratnaprabha's earlobes turned red. She ordered the chauffeur, 'Drive!'

The automobile went away, leaving the lad behind.

But she spotted the youth standing motionless and staring at her and the car again with the same fearless, brazen, curious and astonished eyes. She stared back at him, but he didn't flinch. His gaze had no expectation; it had surprise – pure wonder, infinite astonishment.

Dejected by his neutral gaze, Ratnaprabha ordered the chauffeur to stop the car again. She called the young man and asked, 'How much do you earn out of it?'

'Eight to twelve annas a day,' he said.

Ratnaprabha said, 'Can't you manage without vending these dirty books?'

The youth remained silent.

Brimming with anger, Ratnaprabha said, 'How much for that book?'

'*Kokshastra*? Five rupees only.'

'What is the final price?'

'Two rupees each.'

'Go and fetch all five, you rascal!'

The boy brought all five books. The chauffeur took them. Ratnaprabha threw a ten-rupee note at him and said, 'Beware, don't deal in them from now on.'

Saying this, she threw another note of ten rupees.

On her command, the driver had already started to drive the car and the youth caught the second note mid-flight.

But there was no change in his manner. His gaze remained unchanged and so was the place. His eyes were not ready to bow down. In his stare, there was neither any gratefulness nor any fear. Even politeness was missing.

Stopping the vehicle, she called him once again and said, 'Now what do you peddle?'

He said, 'Whatever you ask for. *Hanuman-Chalisa*, *Tota-Maina*, *Once at Night*...'

'Do you have that book?' asked Ratnaprabha.

'... Yes, shall I fetch?'

Ratnaprabha said in anger, 'You won't change so easily. You need a good thrashing from the police.'

He stood there listening quietly, not uttering a word. His gaze remained unchanged. Ratnaprabha asked, 'How much is your whole stock worth?'

'Twenty rupees.'

Ratnaprabha said, 'Keep twenty-five and drop all of them here. And beware if you do it again!'

The guy brought the books, dropped them in the car and grabbed those notes.

Ratnaprabha said, 'Do you understand? Don't do this business any more. Put up a food stall, do something else. If I see you doing this again ...' And she ordered the driver, 'Drive now!'

But after one or two days the young man was seen vending books again at the same place and staring at Ratnaprabha's car in the same old way. She, however, did not stop this time. But the next day she called and scolded him again, asked him the worth of his stock, which was set at fifteen rupees. She paid fifteen rupees to the youth, then throwing a cane towards her chauffeur, she said, 'Give him a flaying.'

The chauffeur flogged the young man hard around five to seven times. The chap received the whipping in silence but continued to look at Ratnaprabha unflinchingly. A crowd gathered. That's anyway the nature of a crowd. But neither Ratnaprabha nor the youth paid any heed to them. Ratnaprabha asked, 'So, will you ever do it again?'

The youth's expression did not change. Ratnaprabha said, 'Beat him some more. He has not yet understood well.'

The chauffeur obeyed her command as Ratnaprabha held the man's audacious gaze. There was no expectation of mercy in it.

Watching impatiently, she ordered the chauffeur to stop, 'Let it be, he must have got some wisdom now.'

The lad remained still. His eyes were wide, and in them were red threads. As if they were ignorant, somewhat mysteriously. But neither those eyes were wet nor red with anger. They looked in the same way – still, astonished and placid.

Ratnaprabha hastily told the chauffeur, 'Take out the books from the bundle and start the car.' Soon, they drove away.

After this incident, the young man was not seen for almost a week. In a way, Ratnaprabha was unperturbed and felt calm these days. A week later, she found the young man again but not standing and staring or vending anything; on the contrary, he was sitting by the side of the road and singing devotional songs while playing the *dafli*.

He fell silent on seeing her car approach. He resumed singing when the car was gone. His voice was sweet sounding. His vocal cords had melody in them. When he sang, a quiver accompanied his voice, piercing one's heart.

That he sang well became evident to Ratnaprabha when she heard him singing some lines of a devotional composition. It was, as if, she could listen to him without hearing his voice. That day, as she reached the Yamuna, the young beggar's verse and voice were playing in her mind. At the time of prayer, one canto was echoing in her mind, '*Prabhuji more avgun chit na dharo*' (O Lord! Please ignore my vices).

On her way back as she was driving past the young man, she noticed the singing had stopped. Ratnaprabha asked her driver to pull over and said, 'Go and tell him not to stop.'

The chauffeur spoke to the young beggar and returned, but he did not resume his singing.

Ratnaprabha said, 'Go and tell him, does he want to be beaten up again? He should continue singing.'

The chauffeur returned and told the young beggar as much, but he remained silent and did not follow Ratnaprabha's orders. In a rage Ratnaprabha commanded, 'Start the car.'

As soon as the vehicle moved, she heard a canto – '*Samdarsi hai* …'

Ratnaprabha said to her driver, 'Drive slowly, the road is bad, don't you see?'

'*Samdarsi hai … samdarsi hai nam tiharo* …' (You are known as the Impartial One).

She listened to the song from the car and carried this part of the verse back home. She kept on reflecting that his name is the Impartial One. He can love everyone. Everyone is the same before him. One is high, another low. One is beautiful, another ugly. One is in the car, the other on his feet. But everyone is equal before him. '*Oonch-neech sab ek varan bhaye*' (High and low, all become one), she was thinking, and, so it felt, his pulsating sound echoed inside her, '*Samdarsi hai nam tiharo … Prabhuji more avgun chit na dharo*' (You are known as the Impartial One … Lord! Please ignore my vices).

The next morning, the young beggar was at the same spot, singing. As the car stopped, the man stopped. On Ratnaprabha's command, the chauffeur called the young man closer to the car. Ratnaprabha said, 'So, what do you do now?'

'I sing,' he replied.

'*Arey*, what do you do to feed yourself?'

'I beg.'

'Why do you beg?'

The young man stood there without answering.

'Do you get enough alms?'

The man didn't answer.

'Do you ask for bread or money to buy food?'

The young beggar kept looking at Ratnaprabha with an unflinching gaze. He didn't utter a word.

'Will you accept alms from me?'

To this too, he did not reply.

Feeling exasperated, Ratnaprabha said, 'No, not charity, I can give you a *naukri*. Will you do that?'

The lad said, 'I'll.'

'Then sing.'

Again, a crowd had gathered. The beggar continued to stand still. He didn't sing.

Ratnaprabha asked, 'Why don't you sing, if you want a job?'

The beggar once again didn't answer. He kept staring.

Ratnaprabha said, 'You go, then. You better be begging. You are not worth anything else.'

Perhaps, Ratnaprabha expected that the young man would leave. But seeing him standing like deadwood, she scolded her driver, 'Why the hell have you kept the car parked here? Don't stop this way on the street.'

The car left and so did the beggar. He went back to his spot and started singing, '*Mhaane chakar rakho ji, prabhu ji mhaane*' (Employ me as your servant, O Lord, employ me ...).

The beggar's voice travelled to Ratnaprabha's ears. There was a temple a stone's throw away. She heard his voice as she entered the temple on her way back from her visit to the Yamuna. Bowing before the deity, it felt as if she was pleading the same, 'O Lord, keep me with you, I'll be at your service, I'll do your *chakri*, don't let me go anywhere, take me in your shelter!'

On its return, the car did not stop but went straight ahead. For a couple of days, the same routine followed. The young beggar was found singing at the same spot. The first day the singing stopped, so did the second day, but then it was noticed that his singing continued without caring for her passing car. Ratnaprabha wondered, 'Does he even look up to see me now? Perhaps, he is not bothered about it any longer, or is he?'

Letting things go as they had been for four, five days, she again called him through his chauffeur and asked, 'How much will you take to do a job?'

The question remained unanswered. The old gaze had returned to the young beggar's eyes.

Hurriedly, Ratnaprabha asked, 'So, where do you sleep? Do you have more clothes or this is it? Do you get enough alms to cover yourself?'

'I sleep here, anywhere,' he replied briefly.

Ratnaprabha said laughingly, 'Has anyone ever hectored you?'

The man said, 'At times, yes.' He kept staring in his old way.

Ratnaprabha felt embarrassed and said, 'So, you didn't say, how much do you expect from the naukri?'

The lad didn't reply.

Ratnaprabha said in irritation now, 'Tell me honestly, do you want to do the naukri or not? My questions make your temper fly high.'

The young beggar ignored the provocation and said, 'I'll do.'

She asked again, even more annoyed this time: 'So, why don't you say how much wages you want?'

He still didn't reply. Eventually, exasperated and filled with anger, Ratnaprabha said, 'In addition to food and clothing, I won't pay more than fifteen. Will you work?'

'I will.'

'You will have to do all my work and you won't go anywhere without my permission. Is that acceptable to you?'

The man stood mum.

Ratnaprabha continued speaking, 'All of my work, whatever I ask. Washing clothes, cleaning home, polishing shoes, everything. Do you have anyone with you?'

'No one.'

'Parents, relatives, kin?'

'None.'

'How come there is nobody? Where do you belong to?'

The young man kept mum.

'Why do you go silent? Why don't you speak?'

The young man continued to watch her with the same unflinching stare that showed neither respect nor contempt. There was neither a fear of her anger nor an expectation of sympathy. His stare was lifeless.

Ratnaprabha said, 'With these traits you want to do naukri? Go away and continue begging.'

The car drove off and the young beggar, returning to his spot, began to play his tambourine and sing, '*Aey musafir, range dunia chand roj*' (Oh passer-by, paint up the world for few days).

After returning home, Ratnaprabha felt upset with herself. She wanted to punish the beggar boy severely but was unable to decide. Finally, she called the chauffeur and commanded him to present that boy by five o'clock in the evening in a good shape – in decent attire and appearance. 'And, bring along his old stuff, don't throw them away,' she said.

Things happened as she had ordered. The beggar marked his presence before Ratnaprabha in decent guise. He didn't look bad in this appearance.

Ratnaprabha said, 'Oh, you, do you even know how you look? Come and see.' Saying this, she turned him straight towards the mirror. Standing behind him, she herself began to see. She observed that the young man was looking at himself in the same manner as he used to stare at her. His gaze was unprompted and unaffected. It moved away from his own self in the mirror and fell on Ratnaprabha's face. Anticipating a glimmer of hope, Ratnaprabha was overwhelmed for a moment. But on seeing again, she recognized the glare was the same, that of a statue, unmoving like a stone. There was no action, no reaction.

Ratnaprabha moved away and sat on the bed. She said, 'How long will you keep looking in the mirror? Come here.'

The young man turned his face.

'You will have to do all my work. If unacceptable, then better be clear now. Here lies your cassock and your dafli, you can leave even now.'

The young man didn't disagree to doing all her work.

'So, do you also play flute?' she asked.

Taking out the pipe from his bundle, Ratnaprabha gave it to him and said, 'Play something.'

Holding the flute, the young man stood immobile.

'Are you worried about distraction? Let me close the door, nobody will disturb you now!'

Uttering so, she stood up and shut the doors to her room. 'Play.'

The young man kept standing like before, unmoved, and didn't place the flute to his lips.

Ratnaprabha said, 'Haven't I told you that you have to do all my work when you are under my employment?'

The lad said, 'I won't work.'

Ratnaprabha was simply stunned at first. Then, throwing

away his stuff from the table in anger, she shouted, 'This seventy rupees which have been spent on your clothes, tell me now, from which father of yours should I recover, you pauper? So easily you said you won't work! What else will you do? You are destined to eat leftovers, and you deserve to do so.'

The young man continued to stare with his dispassionate eyes. He heard everything, but didn't utter a word.

Ratnaprabha continued to waste her anger for some time. In the end she said, 'Will you do the household chores, washing and cleaning?'

'I'll do.'

'But you won't sing?'

The man stayed silent.

Ratnaprabha said, 'Will you sweep in these clothes? You don't have any regard for the clothes?' Saying this she opened the door and rang the bell.

The same chauffeur came on the ring. She said, 'Listen, take this man along. Send Mangal to the office; he will get his new dress from there. Take Mangal's old pair of clothes back, hand them over to this new guy and explain his work to him. So, what's your name?'

The young man said, 'Don't know.'

Ratnaprabha said, 'You are one mad creature. You don't even know your own name. People must be calling you something?'

'They call me the Little Ascetic (*nanha bairagi*).'

'Little Ascetic!' Ratnaprabha laughed out loud and said, 'Ascetics don't have English hair. Go now, and did you hear, you are not an ascetic. And, he will explain to you your work.'

While leaving, the lad tried to pick up his kit. But Ratnaprabha quipped, 'There is no pearl packed in it that may cause greed in a renouncer! Leave that here. Go and check out your tasks.'

He went off to get acquainted with his work. Ratnaprabha, too, remembered some of her own tasks. She usually remained engrossed in her work and did not clutch onto her wealth. Therefore, involuntarily at this young age, she had been drawn into communitarian services. She was hardly ever free from such engagements. While stepping out and returning home she noticed this man every day (whose name had now become Mangal) sitting on her doorstep in a knee-long dhoti and waiting for her commands. But she did not have time; after glancing at him, she always passed by.

Mangal cleaned her entire house, washed everyone's clothes and even obliged other servants of the household, when asked. This she knew and was satisfied with. One day, while going out, she asked out of courtesy, 'Mangal, are you all right?'

Raising his face, Mangal looked at his mistress. The same eyes, in which there was neither dissatisfaction nor complaint. Unwavering like a rock.

Ratnaprabha asked but moved along without waiting for him to reply, and yet she got upset. Her trouble was that everything was going well. Mangal woke up early, sang devotional hymns and cleaned the entire house before others woke up. Ratnaprabha didn't like any of this.

She called the chauffeur and scolded him, 'Your new

man does not even have the courtesy to stand up properly when I walk by him. Is it for me to teach that as well?'

From then on, it was seen, whenever Ratnaprabha crossed, Mangal bowed down before her in *bandagi*. But it did not lessen her troubles. She felt, it was not a man but a machine that bowed to her.

Around the same time, Ratnaprabha needed to go to Shimla. She had suggested to a women's organization about the necessity of sending a delegation to Shimla, knowing little that the burden of that initiative would fall upon her.

Ratnaprabha called the chauffeur and said, 'A person will have to go to Shimla with me. Who will go?'

The chauffeur said, 'Whosoever you command.'

'How is your new man?'

'He is fit, but he doesn't talk.'

'What will I do with a dumb man? Absolutely silent? But he does his work, he is not a rogue, right?'

'He is still very new, but not ill-mannered.'

'Call him then.'

Mangal came and stood before her as if he were a statue but observing everything with his inner eyes.

Ratnaprabha hastily ordered the chauffeur, 'Go to the office and get an order released for the store to prepare two warm suits. We have to leave on Monday.'

The chauffeur recoiled and said, 'Huzoor, a slip …'

Ratnaprabha said indignantly, 'What's wrong with you? Despite being an old-timer you forget! Am I not saying go and get the order typed and then I will sign?'

The chauffeur bowed and left. Then Ratnaprabha said,

'Mangal! Can you hear? Why don't you talk to anybody?'

Mangal raised his head on hearing her but didn't speak.

'And you don't sing also?'

To this too, he didn't reply.

Ratnaprabha asked, 'Why don't you sing here?'

He continued to stare with the same gaze and didn't speak a word.

Ratnaprabha spoke helplessly, 'You sing well. I like devotional songs. But my devotion has taken a backseat. I have so many other engagements. But what has happened to you? Am I so bad? Do you really hold it against me that I got you thrashed? If you don't like sweeping and cleaning, you can quit. You have not said even once that you don't like it. I have noticed that you don't seem to be grateful enough to acknowledge from which condition I have rescued you … So bad I am … In Shimla, there are forests, trees. Have you ever seen them? You may not have. It is also very deserted there. It is unlike anything here. You can sing there without inhibitions. What are you looking at? You should not look in this manner … Oh, you brought it!'

Taking the piece of paper from the chauffeur Ratnaprabha signed and said, 'Mangal, take this paper and go with him. I shall not be free but we have to depart on Monday. Be ready to leave once I say.'

She lay down on the bed after sending them away. After a long time, she found time to recline on the bed during the daytime. Recumbent, she wanted to fathom her own mind. 'Should I drop going to Shimla? Shouldn't I go alone?' Whirling in these thoughts for some time, she consciously decided that Mangal was an obstinate man and must be brought in line.

In Shimla, she hired a separate mansion and also arranged for a hill servant. She told Mangal, 'You were free, but I had put you in chains. Here, you are not a servant; you can do as you desire.'

He remained unmoved while listening to all this.

Ratnaprabha continued, 'Roam around, stay well and indulge in singing. I have done you an injustice. Are you happy to be free now?'

Neither happiness nor anger appeared on Mangal's face. A new suit was on his body, which appeared stacked on him. When he felt compelled to answer, he said, 'Where is my cassock? If I get it, I'll leave.'

Ratnaprabha asked in a hurry, 'Where will you go? I am not separating you. This dress is yours, the place is yours. Why do you live like a stranger? I say that you are no longer in bounds. You can sing now, play the flute. Look here, I have brought your flute. You stay very lonesome and don't talk. This is not alright. We also live in this world; for you no one matters. Why do you remain so aloof? I am here. I have brought you here. I can do much more for you. What do you desire?'

Listening to all this, Mangal stayed mute – as if he did not understand any of it.

Ratnaprabha continued, 'I haven't seen anyone like you who is so inert – only God knows. *Arey*, why don't you say what you want?'

Ratnaprabha felt that he would forget things before her – as if he did not know where he was! In front of her, he would look baffled all the time. Ratnaprabha would get interested, express annoyance; but she would undergo all these emotions on her own. He on his part would keep standing like a stone.

Ratnaprabha blurted in anger, 'Go, get lost of my sight!'

In a fit of rage, she took out his robe from the trunk and throwing it away said, 'Grab it and get out of here.'

Sunk in disbelief, for some time, the guy watched her motionless. Then, carrying his clothes and flute, he left.

Ratnaprabha continued to watch as the man left but did not say anything. She wanted to scratch herself hard out of fury. Never had she felt such humiliation. She stood up, went to the balcony and continued to watch the uneven hilly slopes spread out in front of her. She found that the young man, wearing his cassock and holding the flute in his hand, was walking away from the mansion. She stood there motionless on her balcony watching as the man walked beyond the hills and slowly merged with the darkness of the dense woods in the distance and disappeared.

Trees, how innumerable are they! In their cavernous shadow, all gets covered. All is lost into them. How deep are these forests! Dark, deep, and quiet. Clouds squat on them, as if everything is mysterious. The forest, waiting despondently – whom is it calling!

Standing there, Ratnaprabha continued watching the dark-shaped vast expanse of the forest that was sprawled over in front of her balcony. As she was getting some kind of invitation from deep inside its successively expanding blackness. But in a flash, she returned to her room and busied herself with her work.

The day had ended. The evening was also almost over. She sighed deeply. She felt relieved. He was destined to leave, so he left. She ordered a cup of tea, and it came. The tea brought about a sense of verve in her. The evening was very cold. Covering herself well with a shawl, she opened the window. Clouds were all over the horizon. Nothing was visible. Invisible clouds coming in through the window were filling the room. She packed her ears as well with the shawl. It was drizzling outside; she prepared another cup of tea and beheld its rising steam.

As night fell, she asked the hill servant about Mangal; she had heard that the he was present there in the house. She did not pay much heed to that. But the guy had taken care of himself. He had his dinner, found a place upstairs, enveloped himself in a blanket and went off to sleep in a corner.

The same routine continued. The young man came in at the time of dining but stayed away during the rest of the day. In fact, he also spent a night or two away.

One day Ratnaprabha asked him, 'You play flute for that hill girl! Is she very beautiful?

The man said, 'She laughs with me.'

'Do you also laugh with her?'

'Yes, I too laugh with her.'

'So, you are not lonesome? Not an ascetic?'

'I am not.'

'But you don't laugh with me. If I laugh with you, then?'

The guy kept mum.

'You won't laugh and you will not play the pipe, am I so bad?'

The man didn't utter a word, he kept staring in his usual manner.

'But I am not a bad woman. If you play the flute, I will listen to it. If you laugh, I will laugh with you. Why do you treat me like this?'

The man remained silent.

Ratnaprabha said, 'Do you love her?'

The lad didn't reply.

'Will you marry her?'

He didn't reply to this either.

'Her family has a condition that you have to settle with her here after the marriage, do you know?'

'I know.'

'So you won't come back with me?'

The man fell silent.

Ratnaprabha, at that moment, called the hill servant and his sister. She said, 'We shall depart tomorrow. You should clear your accounts, and you may go now.'

After they left, Ratnaprabha told the man, 'Now you have to do all the work at this place, and you will definitely come along with me.'

The young man didn't object to anything. Without further instructions or showing protest, he began to do all the chores, from cleaning to cooking. Apart from some work, he didn't go outside, did not even talk.

Ratnaprabha was annoyed by the man's behaviour. He performed all his tasks well. Why be such a man? Like a machine? One time, as she entered the bathroom, she didn't find the soap case at its place. She yelled, 'Where is the soap?'

The lad said, 'It is inside.'

Ratnaprabha said, 'It's not here; find it and bring it to me.'

The young man remained at his spot. From there he said, 'Please look around it must be there.'

Ratnaprabha screamed in annoyance, 'Oh, you blind man, come here and show me where?'

The lad said a little irately this time, 'I am asking you to please look around – it must be somewhere there.'

Opening the bathroom's door with a huge bang, Ratnaprabha said, 'Instead of preaching and making excuses from a distance, it doesn't cross your mind to come in and show me where it is?'

Saying so, she wrapped a towel around her body. The young man came in, stood on his toes and took out the soap case which was slightly tucked behind other things.

Ratnaprabha said, 'There you see, how could have I reached that far behind? And this water! Why are you standing; dip your fingers and check it for yourself. Is it hot? Bring more warm water.'

He brought some more hot water.

'I have told you a million times to not put the bucket so far away from the stand. How will I drag it? Mix more cold water, more. Okay, that's it, stop, stop ...'

The youth left after doing all that he was told. After coming out of the bath, Ratnaprabha felt very discontented, 'How can it go on like this? Where have you lost your mind? Do you keep thinking about that girl? Pay attention to your work.'

It was raining since evening that day. It was pouring heavily, perhaps a thunderstorm was in the forecast. The wind was blowing fast; it was banging hard at the doors and windows.

Ratnaprabha wrapped herself up in a quilt. The wind pierced her with its razor-like sharpness. She called the young help and said, 'Can you make tea at this hour?'

At once, he came back with a cup of tea.

Ratnaprabha said, 'Come and sit. Why are you standing? Come and sit here.'

After profuse requests, the lad brought a stool and sat down. He also took a cup of tea.

Ratnaprabha asked, 'Don't you feel cold? I am shivering even inside the quilt. You have made tea for me at this hour – who are you? A servant never works like this. Tell me honestly, what do you think of me?'

He kept staring at her with wide-open eyes.

Ratnaprabha said, 'Look, no one understands me. That is why I thrashed you – so I am your tough taskmaster. This is the reason I get angry at everyone. If someone is willing to understand me, I can behave normally. I can be sweet-natured. You are making me well. But when you keep mum, it puts me in doubt and I turn bad. I am lonely too. Extremely lonely. You don't sing now – '*Prabhu more avgun chit na dharo*' (O Lord, please don't mind my vices).

The lad continued listening to everything in silence.

'I think of chanting even now that, "O Lord, please don't mind my vices!" I plan, but I don't say, I forget. We all forget. I have so much work. We all forget while being busy in work … Where will you sleep? Is it windy out there?'

'No, it's not.'

'Do you sleep on the floor? Don't you feel cold with a single blanket?'

'No, I don't.'

Ratnaprabha continued staring and then blurted out, 'What wrong have I done to you? Why do you torture me? I am taking revenge on you, are you also doing the same? I recognize you. You are not the same as you appear. When you tolerate everything, hear everything, it can't be that you don't observe any of it. No, no, you do understand everything. Tell me the truth, for I am ill-tempered, do I deserve, therefore, to be paid back in the same coin? You don't get angry. You profess love. Can you claim that you don't love? I see it all in your eyes; come to me, sit beside me.'

The young man feeling compelled, moved and sat near her. With her both hands, Ratnaprabha held his hand and placed it on her forehead. Her forehead was hot to the touch.

'Oh, no, you have a fever.'[2]

Ratnaprabha said, 'I don't have a fever, but you shouldn't leave.'

'Your fever is quite high.'

Saying so, he stood up to rewrap her in the shawl properly so that her ears were covered and, holding her arms, he brought them under the quilt. He added more firewood to the fire.

As he began to leave, Ratnaprabha asked, 'Where are you going?'

The youth said, 'Going to get a doctor.'

Ratnaprabha said, 'No. Wait, first listen to one thing I have to say. Come and sit here.'

At her begging voice, he stumbled and moved to sit beside her pillow.

Ratnaprabha's temperature was rising incessantly. She said, 'Why did you come in such disguise, why? This is not how you conduct an ordeal. But I have recognized you now. I cannot be tricked anymore.'

Saying so, Ratnaprabha placed both her arms onto his feet and continued, 'Haven't you come to put my pride on trial, O you ascetic?' Pushing me high and up, you continued to bow and bend further down. I have understood your game now. I am not going to let you go by falling into your trap, O my silent one. Please make me your servant, my lord, please make me your servant ...'

The young man looked at Ratnaprabha's face nervously. He then stood up, looking frantic.

Holding his hands, Ratnaprabha asked, 'Where are you going, my ascetic? Before you go, please tell that you are not angry and you have forgiven me.'

Looking compassionately into the eyes of helplessly lying Ratnaprabha, the young man balked and stood still.

Suddenly forsaking his hands, Ratnaprabha said, 'You go now, I have found everything in your eyes. Everything, you may go now.'

The guy went to get a doctor at once.

With the doctor's help and his tireless service, he brought Ratnaprabha to full recovery. His hair had grown now and he had begun wearing the cassock as he did earlier. After her recovery, Ratnaprabha said, 'I promise you that I am not going to lose you. Wealth is fickle and the world is meaningless, so penniless devotion is all that a person possesses. I could realize this because of you. So as to displace my pride and let this message stay inside me, I will always keep you in mind. But, as you leave now, won't you play your flute for me?'

For the first time, then, the young man smiled and placed the flute to his lips.

Ratnaprabha became unconscious listening to his flute. When she woke up, the piper was gone.

Blouse

SAADAT HASAN MANTO

Momin was feeling restless for the past few days. His whole being had become like a raw abscess. While working, talking or even thinking, he felt a strange kind of pain, an agony that he could not talk about even if he so wished.

While remaining stock-still he often became flabbergasted; hazy thoughts, which normally appear and disappear like soundless bubbles, entered his mind with a clamour and exploded with a roar. On the soft and delicate sheath of his heart and mind, he felt as if ants crawled with their spiked legs. His organs sensed a weird kind of crick which caused severe ache. When the intensity of the soreness heightened, he felt like throwing himself into a mortar and asking someone to smash his body with a pestle.

While grinding *garam masala* in the kitchen, as the iron of the pestle and mortar drubbed against each other and its trill caused the floor to judder, his bare legs found the twitching sensation soothing. Through his legs, the twitch ran into his tense calves and thighs, and went up to his heart, which trembled like the flicker of a floor-lamp kept open in the wind.

Momin was fifteen, perhaps entering his sixteenth year. He was ignorant of his age, though. He was a hale and hearty boy, whose boyhood was racing towards the peak of adolescence. It was this race, which he was unmindful of, that caused a sensation in every single drop of his blood. He tried to fathom its meaning but failed.

Many changes were evident in his body. His neck, which was slender earlier, was now thick; a muscular twist had emerged in his biceps; his throat had a bulge; a layer of flesh had padded his chest and, of late, his breasts had become roundish and prominent, and bulged as if in them were padded wild geese on each side. He felt severe pain when touched on this growing bulge. Occasionally, while working, if his hands accidentally touched them, he jolted in agony. He felt an ache even when the coarse fabric of his shirt brushed against them.

While taking a bath or working in the kitchen, when nobody else was present, he unbuttoned his shirt, stared at the globules and squeezed them; it pained, it twinged and his entire body trembled as if a fruit-laden tree had been shaken. Yet, he indulged in playing this game that gave him pain. Sometimes, on being excessively pressed, the globules were punctured and a viscid fluid trickled down. Seeing the gooey fluid, his face turned red like his earlobes. And he felt the guilt that accompanied a commitment of sin.

His knowledge of wrong and right was very limited. Anything that a person could not do before another was wrong in his opinion. When his face turned red like his earlobes in shame, he quickly buttoned up his shirt and vowed to never ever indulge in such appalling acts again. Despite his promises, after a couple of days, he nevertheless indulged in the same act in solitude.

Everybody in the house was happy to find Momin to be a hardworking boy. He had been working at the Deputy Saheb's house for barely three months. But in such a short period of time, he had impressed everyone in the household with his industrious nature. He was hired on six rupees a month, but in the very next month of his hiring, his salary was increased by two rupees.

He was also very happy working at Deputy Saheb's house because of the dignity it accorded him. But for the last few days he had felt restless. A strange kind of vagrancy had spurted in his mind – he wished to wander aimlessly in the market or go and lie idle at any isolated place.

He did not enjoy his work anymore. Despite this indifference, he did not shirk his duties. That is why nobody was aware of his inner turmoil. There was Razia, who was always busy playing music, learning newly released film tunes and memorizing the lyrics. She had never paid any attention to Momin. Unlike her, Shakila used Momin for some odd jobs, and at times even rebuked him. But for the last few days, she was also busy copying some blouse samples. These blouses belonged to a friend of hers who was extremely fond of wearing the latest designer dresses. She had borrowed eight blouses from her friend and was replicating their designs on paper sheets. Therefore, she had not paid attention to Momin at all.

Deputy Saheb's wife was not a strict woman. There were two servants in the house, that is, apart from Momin, there was an old woman who mostly worked in the kitchen. Momin assisted her occasionally. Deputy Saheb's wife might have possibly noticed his slackened diligence, but she never enquired Momin about it. Moreover, Deputy Saheb's wife was completely unaware of the upheaval that Momin's mind and body were going through. She had no son, so she could not have gauged Momin's mental and physical changes, and, after all, Momin was a servant – who bothers to care about servants anyway. They walk past many milestones – from childhood into senility – but people around them do not even get a whiff of their arduous journey.

Momin was certainly in the same state. Passing through unknown turns and twists of life for the last few days, he had arrived on a path that was not quite long but undoubtedly uneven. On this road, at times, his footsteps leaped forward, at others they slowed down. He did not know how to march on these roads – whether to stride away quickly or to wait and walk slowly using support to be found along the way. Beneath his naked feet, round and lubricious morsels of youth kept slipping. He was unable to maintain balance and became extremely fretful. Due to this restlessness, he often felt flustered while working and swung himself across by holding a pole with both his hands. In this moment, a desire would swell in his heart; somebody should hold his legs, he felt, and pull them until he morphed into a thin wire ... Similar thoughts emerged in such a remote corner of his mind that he was unable to comprehend their meaning.

Instinctively, he wished for something to happen; what should happen? Just something should happen ... he had no idea. Perhaps some unforeseen circumstance ... decoratively arranged plates on the table might abruptly begin to fly; the steam kettle's cover might blow up in the air; the tap's mouth might expand and break into a fountain; or he may get such a powerful stretch that each of his body joints might get parted, loosening his entire body ... an occurrence, which he had never experienced before.

Momin was terribly fidgety.

Razia was immersed in learning new filmy tunes.

Shakila was duplicating blouse samples on paper sheets. After finishing that task, she kept the best one in front of her and began sewing a purple satin blouse. Now keeping aside her music instrument and song book, Razia, too, had to turn her attention towards Shakila.

Shakila performed all her tasks with fervour and precision. She, unlike her younger sister, Razia, did not appreciate hurry-scurry. While sewing, she made every stitch with utter diligence to avoid any possible mistake. Her skill of measurement was also flawless – first, she would cut along a paper sheet, then run a pair of scissors into the fabric placed in alignment over the paper cutting. It took a lot of time, but the result was impeccable.

Shakila was a healthy girl with a well-developed body; her hands were quite chubby; on each finger joint, at the tip of her meaty conical fingers were little dents. When she ran the sewing machine these dimples disappeared due to the movement of her hands. She even ran the machine patiently. Slowly and eloquently, when two or three of her fingers rotated the machine's handle, a dainty ring appeared on her wrist, her neck tilted a little to one side and a lock of hair, which was unable to find a place for itself, unfurled to the front; Shakila remained so immersed in her work that she didn't even try removing or fixing the hanging locks.

Spreading purple satin when Shakila began to carve a blouse of her size, she recognized the need of an *inchi* tape. Her own tape had thinned out and was badly damaged; an iron *guz* was there, but how could it have been used for measuring her waist and breast? She had a number of blouses, but she had grown slightly plump and she wanted to take fresh measurements.

She had already removed her top for the correct measurement when she remembered that her measuring tape had worn out. She called Momin, and when he came, she asked, 'Momin, go and get a cloth guz from (flat) number six ... Tell them that Shakila Bibi has asked for it.'

Momin's eyes met the white brassiere sticking to Shakila's body. He had seen Shakila in such brassieres before, but this time he felt a sort of hesitancy; he turned his gaze away from her and nervously replied, 'What kind of guz?'

Shakila replied, 'Clothguz ... one type of guz which is lying before you, this is made of iron ... there is also another kind of guz, made of cloth ... go running to flat number six and bring the cloth guz ... tell them Shakila Bibi has asked for it.'

Flat number six was very close to the house. Momin brought the cloth guz quickly.

Shakila took the guz from Momin's hands and asked, 'Stay here ... take it back without delay ...' Then she turned towards her sister Razia. 'If you keep any of their stuff once, that old woman will remind you of the favour a hundred times ... come here, hold this guz and take a measure from this point.'

When Razia started taking Shakila's measurements, a squabble broke out between them. Standing at the door Momin was listening to it in aching silence.

'Razia, why don't you measure by straightening the guz? You did the same mistake the previous time; you took the measurement and my blouse was ruined ... if the blouse does not fit perfectly in the upper part, it droops oddly on the sides.'

'Where to measure and where not to, you put me in a bizarre dilemma ... I began with measuring the upper part, you asked me to move down ... even if a blouse is little tight or a little loose, the heavens will not fall.'

'Oh wow ...! The beauty of the blouse is in the precision of the fitting ... look at Suraiya, how neatly her dresses fit; dare a crease appears on her dresses ... how beautiful such apparels look ... Okay, you take the measurement now.' Uttering so, Shakila drew a deep breath and began to push up her breasts. After swelling up her breasts to her own approval, she held her breath and muttered in a suffocating voice, 'Okay, do it fast.'

When Shakila released the air from her chest, Momin felt the smashing of many rubber balloons inside his body. He uttered nervously, 'Bibiji, give me the guz, I'll go and return it.'

Shakila scolded him, 'Wait a minute.'

As Razia began to measure the circumference of Shakila's arms just below the shoulders, Shakila raised her hands a little.

Momin saw a tuft of dark hair under Shakila's fair armpit. He had noticed similar hair growing under his armpits as well, but he found hers exceedingly pleasant. A sensation ran through his entire body and a weird kind of desire arose in his heart; could that dark hair of Shakila's armpit become his moustache? In his childhood, he used to carve out moustaches from black, brown and golden maize hair. The sensation which he had felt then by stroking cornsilk on his creamy lips, his weird yearning now created the same tickle on his lips.

Shakila had lowered her arms and her armpits were now hidden but Momin could still see those dark hair thickets. In his imagination, Shakila's arms were still up and black hair was still peeping from under her armpits.

After a while, Shakila handed over the guz to Momin and said, 'Go and give it back to them, and tell them that Shakila Bibi has conveyed a lot of thanks.'

Momin returned the guz and sat in the courtyard. Hazy thoughts occupied his mind. For long he tried to make sense of them, but when he failed, he unthinkingly opened his own little trunk in which he had stocked newly stitched clothes for Eid.

As he opened the trunk, the smell of new *latha* filled his nose. He felt an urge to take a bath, wear these new clothes and then go to Shakila Bibi to greet her – how amazing his starched new latha salwar would feel along with his *fez* …

As soon as he imagined the fez, its pom-pom appeared before his eyes and, very quickly, the pom-pom morphed into a clump of the dark hair that he had seen on Shakila's armpits.

He reached out to his fez lying under the pile of his clothes. As he began fondling its soft and tender pom-pom, he heard Shakila call, 'Momin!'

He put the fez back in the trunk, covered it and went inside where Shakila had cut many purple satin pieces in accordance with the sample blouse.

Stacking those slippery pieces at one place, Shakila turned towards him, 'I have called you so many times … Were you sleeping?'

He stammered, 'No, no, Bibiji!'

'Then what were you doing?'

'Nothing … No … Nothing, Bibiji.'

'You must have been doing something!' Shakila continued questioning, but her mind was on the blouse that she was to baste.

With a jeering laugh, Momin replied, 'I was looking at my new clothes stored in the trunk.'

Shakila burst out laughing; Razia joined her, too.

Seeing Shakila laughing, Momin felt a peculiar kind of gratification, and this sense of fulfilment caused a heartful craving to do something silly, though in a funny manner, which would further amuse Shakila. Floundering like a girl, he shyly spoke, 'I will take money from Badi Bibiji and also buy a silk handkerchief.'

Shakila asked in jest, 'What will you do with that handkerchief?'

He replied coyly, 'I'll tie it around my neck, Bibiji … it will look amazing.'

Hearing his answer, Shakila and Razia continued to laugh for long.

'If you tie it around the neck, remember, I shall hang you with the same.' Shakila tried to control her laughter and said to Razia, 'The silly boy completely distracted me … Razia, why did I call him?'

Rajia didn't reply and continued humming a new filmy tune which she had been practising for the past two days.

In a few seconds, Shakila remembered why she had called him. 'Look Momin, I'll remove this vest and give it to you … the new shop near the medical store where you had been with me the other day … go there and ask how much will they charge for six such brassieres … Tell him, I will buy half a dozen, so ask him to give a discount … Do you understand?'

'Yes, Bibiji.'

'Now you move a bit to the other side.'

Momin stepped out and went behind the doors.

After a while, a bra fell near his feet and then came Shakila's voice from inside, 'Tell him I want the same quality, similar design and exactly the same stuff … there should be no difference at all.'

Saying 'all right', Momin picked up the bra, which was slightly wet with sweat as if it has been quickly removed after being left for a while in the steam. The odour of Shakila's body was still stuck to it and so was a sweet warmth. Each of these, he found to be enormously pleasing.

Squeezing the bra, which felt soft like a kitten, he went out.

When he returned from the market after enquiring the price, Shakila had begun sewing the blouse, the same purple satin blouse which felt softer and tender than the pom-pom of his fez.

From the other side of the door, he communicated the price to Shakila and then went to sit in the courtyard.

He thought, perhaps the blouse was being made for Eid as the day of festivities was approaching.

He was called a number of times that day – to bring thread, to take out the iron press ...

In the evening, when Shakila left the remaining work for the next day he was also called to pick up and remove the waste pieces of thread and purple satin.

Momin cleaned the room very well, threw the waste out, but kept the shiny little stripes of purple satin in his pocket, without any purpose – he didn't know what he would do with them. A day later, he took out those little pieces, sitting in a corner, he started unweaving the yarns. He was engrossed in this game for so long that a clump was formed out of the thread slivers. He continued pressing and squeezing the thicket – in his imagination, it was the same armpit under which he had seen the thicket of black hair. That day too, Shakila had called him many a times – all through the day various shapes of the purple satin blouse continued reappearing before his eyes.

First, the blouse was basted and long tacks of white yarn were, therefore, spread all over it; then it was iron-pressed, hence the wrinkles vanished and the shine of the satin doubled up; next, Shakila tried it on herself to show Razia; thereafter, in the other room near the dressing table, she carefully examined herself in the mirror from every possible angle. And when she was absolutely satisfied with its fit and make, she took off the blouse. She marked out the spots that were either too tight or too loose. After rectifying all its glitches, she wore it again. When the blouse fit perfectly well on Shakila's body, she went for the final stitch.

Here, in the room, a satin blouse was being stitched and there, in Momin's mind, the threads of strange thoughts were being untacked.

As he was called in the room, his eyes fell on the shining purple satin blouse; he wished to touch it; not only that, he yearned to caress its soft and furry surface with his hands – his coarse and bristly hands.

From caressing the satin scraps, he had estimated the softness of the blouse – the threads, which he had extracted from those scraps, were soft. When he stretched the thicket of thread slivers, he had felt that the threads were supple like rubber.

Whenever he saw the blouse on entering the room, his mind quickly turned towards those scraps and from there to the hair that he had earlier seen under Shakila's sides. Jet black hair … He wondered whether they were as soft as satin.

Eventually, the blouse was ready.

He was sweeping the floor with a wet cloth when Shakila entered the room.

Shakila removed the top she was wearing and dropped it on the bed. Under it she was wearing the same kind of white bra that Momin had carried as a sample to the market. She then wore her self-stitched blouse over the bra, fastened its front hooks and stood before the mirror.

Wiping the floor, Momin looked up into the glass.

The blouse was alive now; in a couple of spots it shone as if the satin had turned white.

Shakila's back was turned on Momin. On her back, because of the blouse's perfect fit, a long patch of midrib was visible.

He could not resist himself; he said, 'Bibiji, you have beaten the tailors also.'

Shakila became very happy at his adulation, but she was keen to know Razia's opinion. So, merely uttering, 'Isn't it good!', she ran out.

He kept on staring into the mirror – he felt that a dark and shiny reflection of the blouse was still lingering in the mirror.

At night, when he entered Shakila's room to put the water jug, he saw the blouse dangling from a wooden hanger by the door.

Nobody was present in the room.

Moving forward, he looked at the blouse carefully; in spite of the fear, he stroked it with his right hand. Stroking it, he felt as if someone was caressing his soft body hair like a breeze.

When he slept at night, he saw many absurd dreams.

Deputy Saheb ordered him to crush a huge mound of coal. As he picked and hammered one hefty piece, it transmuted into a soft and delicate clump of hair ... That lump was actually made up of infinitesimal strings of jaggery that were ball shaped ... Then this ball mutated into a black balloon and began to fly in the air ... After flying high the balloon burst ... and then came a storm and the pom-pom of his fez disappeared ... He went out in search of the pom-pom ... He wandered in known and unknown locations ... All of a sudden, the scent of new cotton began to appear from somewhere ... Then, unknowingly his hand fell onto a black satin blouse ... For a while, he continued to stroke an unseen palpitating substance.

Suddenly, Momin woke up in flurry. For a while he could not understand what it was, and why it was so. Then he felt fear, wonder and a peculiar sting. His condition was inexplicable; first he felt troubling exhaustion and then, after a few seconds, a cold wave crawled over his body.

On the Boil

UPENDRA NATH 'ASHK'

As the boiling milk spilt over the burning charcoal with a hissing sound and its sharp smell filled the air, Chandan hurriedly moved his hand towards the cooking pot, which was red-hot due to the coal burning under it. Chandan helplessly looked around, but there was no piece of cloth to be found. He wished he could sprinkle water on the boiling milk but then realized he had just dipped his flour-full hands and washed them with the water stored in the *lota*. The milk continued to boil; the noxious whiff of its foam filled the room. In the next room, his master and mistress were talking softly. In such a moment of helplessness and hurry, Chandan's hands accidentally knocked the pot off the fire and onto the floor. Chandan's fingertips were burnt. The boiling milk fell on his hands and because of the singe, a painful sigh escaped his lips.

While bringing the pan hastily to the floor, a little milk had spilt on the surface. He cleaned it with the same flour-mixed water and ran towards the bathroom flinging his fingers, as if to hurl the blisters out.

Keeping his hand under the stream of running water, he twitched his face lightly and smiled. Actually, upon doing anything silly this is how he used to shake his head, and a smile curving from the left corner of his lips would reveal a set of teeth through the slit.

The truth was that after putting the milk on the hearth he had started eavesdropping on the conversation between his master and mistress. Although it was quite late in the day and Chandan had already prepared the dough for lunch, they were still engrossed in their tête-à-tête lying in bed, and just a little while ago, his master had ordered him to make tea.

He had put the milk pot on the hearth and had begun to listen in on their chat. Ever since his master got married, he had become reluctant to rise early in the morning. Earlier, he often went for a morning walk, but upon the arrival of his newly wedded wife, he slept with her till late in the day. When awake, he would order Chandan to make tea, and then both of them, the husband and the wife, continued to chat – sweet, playful chat.

Chandan had started enjoying listening to their talk. They talked softly lying on the bed inside, and he tried prying into their conversation sitting outside.

The boiling milk was slowly swelling in the pan due to the high heat, and the inattentive Chandan was immersed in snooping on the couple's heart-to-heart conversation.

'I become helpless, your cheeks are responsible ...'

'Aren't your hands guilty ...'

'Your cheeks are so beautiful that ...'

'They are burning because of your rubs ...'

'Okay, I'll cool them off as well ...'

And Chandan felt that a delicate flower had fallen on a silky soft surface. He visualized his master bringing his lips to his wife's cheeks. Sitting there, his body began to heat up, his organs stiffened and he replaced his master with himself in his fantasies.

After washing his hands, he again shook his head and went inside the store with a smirk. He put a few drops of mustard oil on the blisters that had appeared on his dark skin. Then, he returned to the kitchen and put the kettle back on the hearth.

But even after singeing his hands and jerking his head twice at his stupid conduct, his ears went back towards the bedroom. His imagination started assisting what he heard with absolute dedication, and soon several images began emerging and dissolving before his eyes.

'Chandan!' His master shouted and then asked, 'Have you been dead out there?'

He came back to his senses on hearing his master's voice. Putting together tea and toast in a hurry, he carried them inside.

His master and mistress remained in bed like before. Though they were not in an embrace, leaning on their pillows, they were lying extremely close to each other. The quilt was up to their chests and the master's arm was still under the mistress' neck.

'Keep it here.'

Chandan put the tray on the table.

Looking at him, the master asked, 'What has happened to you? Where is the jug of milk?'

'*Ji*, I'll bring it right away.' And he went towards the kitchen yanking his head and smiling from the left corner of his lips.

Although he brought the milk the very next moment, he still had to bear reprimands as this time around his master found the sieve missing.

Chandan brought the sieve and stood there for a moment. His slanting gaze fell on his mistress' face – the beautiful and fragrant curls of loose hair were scattered on her white, soft and chubby face; her lips looked juicy despite being parched; her smiling eyes had a thin veil of drowsiness; and there was a dainty shadow of lethargy on her face. His master spoke with great affection, '*Jaan*, please prepare the tea!'

But, 'Jaan' sulkily turned away.

'I am asking: won't you have tea?' The master said adoringly and in a tone of persuasion.

'I don't want any tea!' The mistress replied, rubbing her cheek which had been patted tenderly by his master just a little while ago.

The arm under her neck moved and the lady was squeezed in the master's tight hug.

'What are you doing, don't you feel any shame?'

Chandan's heart began throbbing and his master's guffaw filled the room.

'Please, get up, and prepare the tea!' Slackening his grip around his wife's neck, the master said fondly, 'Your cheeks are so appealing that one is tempted to pat them involuntarily.'

The mistress again turned away, wriggling in agony.

'Chandan, you prepare the tea!'

Chandan somehow managed to prepare a cup of tea with trembling hands.

His master took the cup, squeezed 'Jaan' to his side and placed the cup close to her lips.

When he lay down in his room after finishing the household chores in the noon, it was either the effect of the word 'Jaan' or his master's embrace of his wife in his presence, the picture of Johra Jaan swirled before Chandan's eyes. And, involuntarily, he clinched a tattered, dirty, coverless pillow soaked in dirt and oil in his arms.

Like the sudden spill of the boiling milk, this image of Johra mysteriously and unknowingly resurrected itself from the buried caves of his childhood memory. The same short height, voluptuous body, large playful eyes, paan-drenched ruddy lips, heavy hips, bulging breasts and an exactly similar terrific and memorable smile – the origin point of her smile, whether it began from her eyes or her lips was indiscernible.

He was very young those days. He lived with his aunt, for he was an orphan. His aunt worked as a wet-nurse for a seth's children. This seth ran a shop of gramophone and other musical instruments in Chawri Bazaar. Opposite his shop was Johra's *chaubara*, where the earnings of the seth, from the sale of instruments which further changed forms into silver coins, slowly trickled into.

Chandan would sometimes go along with his cousin and the seth's elder son to Johra's chaubara. Johra adored Sethji's son, treated him with sweets and other stuff; the two brothers also received some portions of leftovers. Quite often, when he was playing with other kids in the courtyard beyond the chaubara, Sethji would drop by. He would sit beside Johra, take her in his arms or put his head on her soft thighs.

His master's wife also strikingly resembled Johra – similar short height, heavy hips, raging breasts, round and juicy cheeks, big smiling eyes and rosy lips. Who could have doubted that in that moment of seeing her in his master's embrace, Chandan would not be reminded of Johra.

Immersed in his fantasy, Chandan reached Johra's chaubara and rested his head on her lap as the Seth used to, and imagined Johra adoringly running her fingers through his hair. He forgot that he was soiled up to his knees and that the skin on his legs was dry and cracked. That his blue shorts (once given by his master) had turned black due to dirt. That there was an ugly scar on his dark forehead. That his lower lip was slit and his hair dry, rough and short. He lay in ecstasy as Johra continued caressing his hair. Lying down, having his head on her lap, he turned to her side and wanted to say, 'Johra, how beautiful you are ...!' But some sharp stuff pricked into his waist and he realized he was lying on the bare floor. The stuff underneath his head was not Johra's lap, but the same dirty and greasy pillow.

Chandan yanked his head off the pillow, but this time he did not smile. He got up and sat leaning against the wall. Many years flew before his eyes.

After offering his entire property to the 'beauty' of Chawri Bazaar, Sethji went back to his ancestral home, which was still stuck in the depth of illiteracy and malice, somewhere in central Punjab. Chandan's aunt went back to her village in the principality of Alwar. At this tender age, Chandan became a servant in the house of one of Sethji's friends at a monthly wage of three rupees.

Subsequently, his life became like an old blanket, which one keeps altering but can never fix completely. One mends one corner only to find holes in another.

After finding the current master, he did feel relieved. He felt that he had not met such a cheerful, large-hearted and open-minded master in the last twelve years of his service. But the same boon of open-mindedness turned into a bane for him. His master showered love on his wife, fondled her and often kissed her in his presence. As if Chandan was not a human being made of flesh and blood, but a dough of clay.

Chandan thought – how peacefully he lived before this wedding. This heat in his body, stiffness in his veins, such restlessness and sleeplessness he had never felt before. Earlier, while sleeping, he was oblivious of anyone walking past him. Since the time his master got married and his new mistress arrived, his sleep had gone for a toss. He had strange dreams. The previous night, he had seen Kasni, who was the daughter of his former master. Her bosoms were like unripe pear. Wearing a *lehanga* that ended above her knees and a waistcoat, she would roam around bare-headed. It was the same girl who had come in his dreams and lain next to him. How? Where? He did not remember a thing. But he had awoken. His body was hot, his veins were strained and he was sweating – he could not sleep again.

Not able to fathom anything, he jerked his head over his stupidity, but this time it was no longer funny, and his smirk had disappeared. His master had gone to the office. The mistress was fast asleep inside. He got up and marched towards the room of Jethu – a servant of Rai Saheb, the neighbour. All the servants in the adjoining area used to assemble there during the noon hours.

The full moon of Chaitra was rising behind the gulmohar tree. Sliver dew-drops were shining on the leaves of a young acacia tree leaning on the mansion's wall. Chandan walked slowly out of the room. Bougainvillea's red blooming flowers, which were spread on the mansion's porch, appeared maroon in the moonlight. In a corner, an old jacaranda tree (last year its trunk was axed from the middle) was jigging with bunch of flowers on a few of its branches. From a distance these bunches appeared like tiny little pieces of clouds. The inebriating fragrance of *kakraunda* and *khatta* flowers had seeped into every pore of the environment. Although everyone slept inside the room till now, the arrival of the new year had weakened the cold. Chandan disinterestedly went and stood beneath a small *gondani* tree. Lost in his thoughts, he plucked a couple of gondani fruits and put them in his mouth. They were not fully ripe. His taste was spoiled. In a state of woolliness, he kept standing there for a moment. Then he went to the veranda and very carefully opened the doors to the drawing room.

His bedroom was adjacent to the drawing room and was mostly left open. Usually, he locked one of the entries to the drawing room from the outside while his master bolted the second from the inside. He opened the doors without making any noise. There was a dim light in the master's bedroom; its reflection fell on the door glass. It looked as if someone has painted the door glass with a brush dipped in a mottled light. Stepping on the rug, Chandan slowly moved forward and stood on his toes near the door.

Inside, a red electric bulb was hanging from the ceiling. He started staring hard in its dim light. But he turned his back in the very next moment. His body was heating up, organs were turning stiff, his throat and lips were drying up; something akin to milk was on the boil in his veins.

He rushed out of the room running on tiptoes. He shut the door softly behind him and stood out in the moonlight. The jacaranda's trunk stood before him. He wished to flatten it with the force of his young breast.

In the lawn opposite the house, the innumerable flower plants in multiple colours were prancing beside the fountain. Drops of water were gliding down from their broad leaves. The aroma of kakraunda had further filled the atmosphere. Chandan turned the fountain faucet on. Sweet silver drops of water sprinkled on him.

Why did he go to Jethu's place? He began to think – in the afternoon, servants from nearby households used to gather in Jethu's room. They either played cards or at times gambled on *chausar*, the Indian board game, or mimicked their masters and mistresses occasionally. Sometimes Jethu borrowed the gramophone from his uncle, which he had purchased at a clearance sale from a waste collector. Its sound was like the sob of a diarrhoeal child. Yet they enjoyed listening to songs such as 'On your white smooth cheek o baby' or 'My eyes are interlocked with your eyes'. Recently, Jethu had bought Charlie's new record and all through the afternoon in his room …

तेरी नज़र ने मारा।
एक दो तीन चार पाँच छःसात आठ नौ दस ग्यारह
तेरी नजर ने मारा!

Your eyes have crushed me,
One, two, three,
Your eyes have slayed me

… the song played. Chandan had never gone to Jethu's room. He had no time. Early in the morning his master would wake him up. Chandan massaged his body, prepared his bathwater, made tea for him, cooked a meal after he had left for his workplace, went to his office to deliver the lunchbox; he then came back home, took his bath, ate and slept. He often slept deep and long until dusk; at times his master kicked him out of his slumber when he returned from work. But today, defeated by his sleeplessness, when he had gone to Jethu's room, he heard such stories that even his forty winks went away.

The first touch of drizzle caused his body to shiver. He panicked – what if he caught fever? The season was changing and here he was standing under the fountain and getting wet. What if he caught pneumonia! He yanked his head away at once, but did not smile. Leaving the fountain running, he went to his room and lay down.

Soon his eyes were open. His head was heavy. His body was inflamed and his eyes were bitter and swollen. He had again seen a dream – a bunch of unripe pears were roving around him. Standing in a deserted and lonely building he was trying to grab them. A water tap was running nearby and a child standing close to it was shouting, 'Don't break my toys, don't break my toys!' He turned his head towards him. That child became Kasni and Chandan listened to a pleading voice – 'Don't pluck my pears, don't pluck …'

Chandan stood up in a frenzy. Jethu's voice echoed in his ears. He put on his kurta. He grabbed an old wallet from a dirty and worn-out clay pot, and put it in his pocket. He latched the room and slowly moved out of the house.

Moonlight was spread on the parade-ground like a silver *shamiana*, and the neem trees on the roadside appeared to be holding the moonlight straight. The light of an electric bulb shone through the leaves of the trees, as if a campfire was lit behind the row of those trees.

Chandan reached the Queen Mary Road. A breeze blended with the smell of kakraunda, khatta and *maulshri* was blowing. The shadows of the trees, dotted with moonlight, wavered like a net of light and shade.

He stopped at the chawk of Tis Hazari, hoping to get a tram, but it was already past eleven o'clock. The road was completely deserted. A waste-carrying vehicle drove past spreading noxious fumes. Chandan was irked. He ran across to the Mithai bridge. The raised platform near which the traffic police used to stand was damaged. Perhaps, a car driver had avenged himself over a constable's unjustified anger. The bridge was absolutely desolate. The moon was shining right above it. Beneath the bridge, railway tracks were visible and, at some distance in the gaping darkness, red and green signals were blinking. Chandan leaned his head on a wall of the bridge and, for a while, kept watching the serpentine tracks and twinkling signals in awed silence. Then he walked ahead.

The road was totally abandoned, shops on both the sides were closed and on the footpath some shopkeepers were sleeping on their dirty mattresses. In the light of the full moon, their white bodies shone in their soiled dhotis. Opposite Telivara, on the footpath towards the left, lay a broken horse cart as well as a couple of empty waste-carts. Beyond that, there ran a long whiteish boundary wall; occasionally, from behind it came the sound of the fast running trains. Outside the shops on the right were lying bundles of bamboo sticks, folded cots and empty wooden boxes. Engrossed in his thoughts, Chandan silently reached the Qutub Road's square.

Sadar Bazaar was completely closed. Only the corner sweet shop was open. Chandan's agitated mind had almost calmed down by the time he reached the corner. He only had a feeling of curiosity left in his mind. In the same state, he drank half a litre of hot milk at the sweet shop.

He marched further as if infused with a renewed passion.

Shops were closed on both sides of the road. On the left stood Mashaallah Hotel, which would generally be so choked with customers in the evening that two people would be forced to share a chair, but right now it looked dead with inactivity. A servant of the hotel was eating on a dirty bench. Close by, the barbers' and paan shops were open. In a hair-cutting salon, where a hair-dyer would sit on the wooden plank during the daytime, a labourer, who perhaps did not get any free time during the day, was getting his head tonsured.

Chandan stopped at the tail end of Kath Bazaar for a while. A couple of *tongawallah*s were still hovering around near the assembly point of *tonga*s. The moon was shining exactly at the top of the tonga-shed. Smoke and dust had sullied its glimmer. He entered Kath Bazaar and looked up in astonishment at a chaubara where a beautiful woman was sitting in front of a gaslight. Chandan's gusto was reignited, but the plaza downstairs was still crowded. It was impossible for him to initiate the 'deal' under bright lights and in the presence of a crowd. He looked into the rooms below. In front of each room a stained and soiled curtain was hanging, in front of each curtain was a lamp and in front of each of them was a lady, standing or sitting.

Every now and then, the doors of these rooms closed, and the lady of the room, carrying the lamp, went behind the curtain following a man. For a moment Chandan felt his passion sinking. He moved away and sat, as if for support, on one of the chairs, which lay unfolded at the centre of the plaza. Next to the chair stood a masseur boy who had a collection of colourful bottles displayed on a table.

'Want to get a head massage?'

Chandan nodded uncertainly. Nearby, a similarly bedecked shop was on display. Across that shop on a sprawling veranda, the prostitutes, trading in beauty (although it was difficult to call them beauties) and chastity, were standing in front of their rooms and inviting their customers. To avoid fatigue from standing for long hours or to be better able to display their bosoms, they held on to ropes that were fastened to the ceiling.

As the boy poured oil to massage Chandan's head, he felt a mushy sensation, and the barber boy began his massage. After oiling, he wiped Chandan's head and shoulder, with an extremely dirty towel, and then combed his hair.

When Chandan began to leave from there, he smelt the pungent odour of a cheap scented oil and his zest was back. Leaving the plaza, he veered into an alley. It was neither very crowded nor very brightly lit. He walked till the other end of the street and returned. He was clueless how to initiate a deal. He could not even look into the women's eyes. A bare thought unnerved him. He decided to go back. He should have come with Jethu. He thought of crossing the lane and returning via another route. But he also did not want to go back after coming this far. At that moment a pale, fat woman sitting before a room in the dark eased his difficulty. Two young girls were lying on the carpet next to her. They were exactly of Kasni's age. 'Hey, come, come here,' she called him affectionately.

Chandan went ahead.

She asked in a very soft voice, 'Come, what are you thinking? Twelve annas only.'

The gesture came from the same woman who was sitting on the iron chair in front of the room wearing only a dark blouse and a black sari, whose underarm hair was visible and whose loose breasts were hanging like a pair of cucumbers.

Chandan instead looked at the girl who was lounging on the floor with desirous eyes. There was a little ring in her nose as well. He had heard from Jethu that among this group, the nose ring was the mark of virginity.

Reading his mind, the fat woman said, 'She is very young now – what will she know about these matters?'

Unripe pears danced around Chandan's mind, then danced Kasni, and then again the unripe pears.

And the fat woman said, 'Two rupees.'

Chandan remained silent. He wanted to say, 'Two rupees is too much.'

Then the fat woman said, 'Okay, one and a half rupees. Come on, she still has her nose ring on.'

The milk began boiling in Chandan's veins. His body began to heat up. The next moment, he was behind the dirty, soiled curtain, and behind him was the fat woman with the lamp and the girl.

A week later, Chandan was standing on the porch with his bag and baggage mounted on his head, and inside the room his master was ordering his wife – 'I am sending for a doctor now. Get the whole house cleansed. The rascal has entered every part of the house.'

And, in a forsaken state, Chandan was thinking, 'But that girl was not even thirteen, and she was still a virgin.'

Bahadur

AMARKANT

All of a sudden, I turned sombre like someone should when burdened with an inordinate responsibility. There he was, standing before me, eerily fluttering his eyes. Twelve or thirteen years old, short and stout, fair and with a flat face, he was wearing a pair of white shorts, a short-sleeved white shirt and old brown shoes. A handkerchief was tied around his neck like that of a boy scout. Members of my family stood surrounding him. Nirmala's delighted gaze flitted between the boy, her brother and me. She was certainly overjoyed.

My *sala saheb* had brought him. A servant had become an absolute necessity for innumerable reasons. All my brothers and other relatives were well placed and every one of them had a servant. When I visited home for my sister's wedding, I had witnessed the comfort servants could provide. Both my *bhabhi*s enjoyed queenly indolence, while Nirmala was full of drudgery as she worked without break from morning until night. I fumed with jealousy at their comfort. No sooner was I back at my place and had joined work, Nirmala too could not stop chanting our need for *naukar-chakar*. Was there a woman in this world as wretched and cursed as her? Those are indeed different creatures altogether who are lucky to enjoy the luxury of servants …

First of all, I was forced to listen to my sala saheb in incredible detail. The boy whom he had brought over was a Nepali from a village on the Bihar–Nepal border. His father had died in the war and his mother was the sole breadwinner of the family. The mother was ill-tempered and used to regularly beat him up badly. The mother wanted the boy to help her with household chores, but he wandered off in the mountains or the jungle, climbing trees, catching birds in their nests, plucking and eating fruits. Sometimes he took the animals out for grazing. On one such occasion, he flogged a buffalo that he greatly despised as this animal was his mother's darling. The badly beaten buffalo ran towards his mother who was busy working not far away across the field. The mother grew suspicious – why else would the poor and speechless animal quit grazing and come running to her? She guessed that it must have been brutally beaten by the lad. She was enraged. When the boy came back, she calculated the marks of the beatings on the buffalo, then caned him doubly and left him crying in the field. Something snapped inside him, and the boy was done with his mother. He spent the night hiding in the jungle and at dawn went home stealthily. He took two rupees from the stash of notes kept in the ghee pot and ran away. Six kilometres away, there was a bus stop where one could catch a bus to Gorakhpur.

'What's your name?' I asked.

'Dilbahadur, Saab.'

There was a sweet, singsong ring to his voice. I do not exactly remember what instructions I gave him. Perhaps I asked him to shun mischief, work diligently and treat the place as his own. I also told him that in this house naukar-chakar are treated with love and dignity; whatever everybody eats and wears, the servants are allowed to the same. If he stayed here, he would learn good manners and to read and write just like the boys of the household. And so, his life would be reformed. Nirmala also in that moment added some practical lessons, warning him against the many lowly beings who live in the neighbourhood. He must not visit any such folks and should refrain from doing any work for them. If one of them were to assign him a task, such as to fetch something from the bazaar, he should reply 'I'll soon be with you', and immediately slip back home. Meanwhile, he ought to address all members of the household with respect and maintain the decorum. As such, many more things she preached. Finally, Nirmala, quite generously, clipped the word 'Dil' from the boy's name.

Despite the reservations, Bahadur, turned out to be very cheerful and industrious. For the first few days the atmosphere in our home was exhilarating, as usually happens when you domesticate a puppy or a nightingale for the first time. From early in the morning, small children from the neighbouring houses used to gather inside our place, laughing at Bahadur and asking him odd questions: 'Hey, what do you guys call a lizard?' 'Have you seen a lion?' He was requested to sing songs from the mountains.

My family members also teased him in similar ways. He laughed more than he talked. Everyone made sure he was well fed.

Intending really to be overheard by the neighbours, Nirmala often shouted in the courtyard: 'Bahadur! Why don't you come and have breakfast? I am not like the other women who squeeze their servants dry. I keep my domestic help as I do my own children. My husband has clearly said that the boy must not face even one iota of trouble, no matter if we spend as much as a hundred or one hundred fifty rupees per month on him. We got him a pair of new shorts and a shirt just the other day … and more clothes are being stitched.'

Gradually, he took over all the household work. After rising early in the morning, he would pluck *datun* from the neem tree to brush his teeth. Barely grabbing onto the bark, he ran more than halfway up the trunk. The next moment he was on top of the tree. Beating her breasts, Nirmala shouted at the top of her lungs: 'Oh, you of a monkey's caste, how bad will it be if you fall down!' He cleaned the house and swept the floor, lit the oven, made and served tea. At noon he washed clothes and cleaned the kitchen utensils. He insisted on cooking, but Nirmala cooked vegetables and rotis herself. He was extremely attentive towards Nirmala. She was not keeping well for some days and was on medication. If he saw her working, Bahadur used to say, 'Mataji, please do not work hard; your suffering will increase.' No matter what he was doing and where, at the stipulated hour, he would wash his hands and run like a bear to Nirmala, setting the medicine box in front of her.

On my return from the office, all my family members would come to me and share their experiences of the day. Later he would also join. After looking at me once, he would lower his head and smile sweetly. Then he would recount some totally unremarkable event: 'Babuji, a friend of Bahinji came.' Or, 'Babuji, Bhaiya went to the cinema.' After such reports he would laugh as if he had said something very amusing. His laughter was very soft and sweet like a rain of blossoms. I always wanted to chitchat with him, but instead of acting on my wish, I would become serious and turn away.

Sometimes, Nirmala would ask him, 'Bahadur, do you remember your mother?'

'No.'

'Why not?'

'Why did she beat me?'

After this reply, he would laugh as if getting beaten had been a pleasant experience.

'Yet you ask us to send your money to your mother?'

'Parental debts are to be paid lifelong.'

Then he would laugh even more.

Nirmala had given him a tattered carpet. He had also brought a sheet from his home. After finishing all his work, at night, he made his bed on a broken bamboo cot on the veranda. He would sit on his bed, then take a round Nepali cap from his pocket and wear it. The cap slanted heavily to the left. Next, he would take out a small mirror and, looking into it, would make faces like a monkey. He appeared very happy. Many other things would soon emerge from his pockets to adorn his bed – some small marble balls, an old pack of playing cards, beautiful coloured pebbles, pen knives, paper boats and so on. He would play with them for a while, then start humming some tunes. We did not understand the meaning of those hill songs, but a sweet melancholy would spread through the house as if someone was calling for his long-lost friend in the solitude of the mountains.

~

Time passed happily. The rainy season was already here. It rained and then it stopped, and I felt my spirits rise. I had always been proud of the greatness and *shan-ban* of my family and relations. Now I started looking down upon people in my neighbourhood even more than I had done earlier. I stopped being polite to them. In fact, I did not even give them a normal glance. I would scold and scream at their kids at their most innocuous mischief. Many times, I had declared to my neighbours that only people with large hearts could afford to keep a servant these days. A servant should be, as Bahadur was, kept like kin of the family. Nirmala had also disseminated this news throughout the mohalla: 'Half of our money is spent on the servant; for what purpose is money earned after all? My husband told me many times that he would bring me a servant from any corner of the world ... And he did it.'

Undoubtedly, everyone was enjoying great comfort because of Bahadur. The house was speckless clean, our clothes, bright and white. Nirmala's health also improved greatly. Nobody now did an iota of housework. If someone had even the most minor requirement, he would shout: 'Bahadur, get me a glass of water.' 'Bahadur, my pencil is lying on the floor, pick it up.' Commands of these types! Bahadur danced like a bobbin in the whole house. We all went to bed early at night and did not get up before eight in the morning.

My eldest son, Kishore, was convinced that it was right to live in pomp and show and keep others in awe of himself. So, he had already felt the need to bring Bahadur under the wings of his strict disciplinary regime. Consequently, he transferred all his tasks onto the boy. His shoes were to be polished in the morning. It was necessary that his bicycle be cleaned before he left for college. His clothes should be washed and ironed daily. And regularly before going to bed, he should get a body massage from Bahadur. In the delivery of this endless litany of summons, sometimes instances of non-compliance would occur. In such cases, Kishore would yell and hurl abuses at Bahadur, and even slap him. Bahadur would then go and stand in a corner—silently.

'You see,' Kishore would warn him, 'my tasks should be done first. If you fail to do even one, I'll beat you like hell. You lazy ass, what else do you do all day? You only sit idle and eat.'

Gradually, such events became a daily phenomenon; my wife reported them to me. I forbade Kishore from treating the boy in this way, but when he did not listen to me, I ignored the situation. I reasoned to myself that a little bit of this sort of conflict was normal. And anyway, it takes two to tango. Bahadur, too, must have erred to instigate such behaviour from Kishore. But one day, when I returned from office, I saw Kishore beating Bahadur with a stick. From a distance, Nirmala was shouting and motioning him to stop.

I rebuked Kishore and separated them. Apparently, Bahadur had forgotten to clean his bicycle in the evening. When Kishore became abusive and hit him, Bahadur refused to do his work.

'Why didn't you clean his bicycle?' I asked him sternly.

'Babuji, why did Bhaiya drag my father into it?' he replied tearfully.

I knew that Kishore used to abuse him terribly. But today he had simply called him 'son of a pig', and Bahadur could not take it. Undoubtedly, this abuse was aimed at his father. Unintentionally, I laughed. Despite this, it was clear that Kishore's behaviour was far from good, but being the master of the house, I, too, had my compulsions.

'Bahadur, these are not good habits,' I explained. 'If you work properly, nobody will say anything to you. Working hard is indeed a very good thing; those who shy away from their tasks cannot do any good in their lives. I do not like those who are sulky and irascible. You are just like one of the boys of this house. Don't they get beaten up, too? The way we keep you with kindness and comfort, would anyone else match up to that? Go and check in other households, you will realize it yourself. Servants crave for meals that would justly fill them up. Anyway, all is sorted, go and work now ...'

He listened to all this in silence. After washing his face, he went to do his chores. Soon he appeared happy, too. After going to bed that night, he put on his cap and kept singing for a long time.

A few days later, however, another crisis took place. Nirmala liked to make very thin rotis, so she did not assign this task to Bahadur. But a woman in our mohalla convinced Nirmala that after making rotis for her family members she should ask Bahadur to make rotis for himself. The servants get spoiled otherwise; such dietary delicacy ruins their habits.

This advice appealed to Nirmala and she experimented with it the very same evening. She came out of the kitchen after making her rotis. Bahadur's face turned gloomy. He stood near the oven with his head bowed.

'Hey, what's the matter'? asked Nirmala.

He did not reply.

'Make your rotis without causing a fuss. Do you think that I would feed you my soft and thin rotis? Are you a boy from this family? Servants should cook their own food. Lo and behold! His highness is bitter because I made rotis for the entire household and not for him. Why did I discriminate and exclude him? Wow, this one has a demanding stomach! Let it be clear now, if you do not make your own rotis, you will go hungry. Do you get it?'

As Bahadur continued to stand and sulk, Nirmala grew angry. She jumped up and slapped him round the head a couple of times, 'You pig! This is why you get beaten by Kishore. This is why your mother must have thrashed you. Go and make your own rotis.'

'I shan't make anything … My mother, too, used to do the same. After making rotis for everyone, she told me to make my own.' He started crying.

'Do you think that I am your mother that you can demand this from me? Do you aspire to be equal to the boys of this household? I will beat you black and blue.'

But Bahadur did not make rotis for himself. I was also very angry. I scolded him and reasoned with him. But he did not budge. He went hungry that night.

In the morning, however, he carried on cheerfully just like usual. He lit the firewood and made his rotis. He giggled at his thick and ugly rotis. Then he ate them with the leftover curry.

Nirmala's hand, too, however, had lost its control now. She was generally irritated by him. She slapped him even on his faintest mistake. There were two people to beat him at home now. Sometimes both mother and son thrashed him for the same fault.

The monsoon was over. The sky was clear as a mirror. I had written a letter to Bahadur's mother stating that her son was happy with us and that I would send his salary to her. But even after months there was no reply. I told Bahadur that his money would remain deposited with me; he could take it whenever he left for home.

But Bahadur's faults and errors were on the rise. Perhaps the reason for this were the beatings and abuse. Sometimes I wanted to intervene but remained silent thinking that servants do get beaten anyway.

On one Sunday, a relative of my wife visited. He had his wife and children with him. Although they had come to see another close relative, they dropped in at our place as well. The house was suddenly full. I bought some *rohu* fish and Dehradun rice. After breakfast, an endless tittle-tattle began. Meanwhile, an unexpected event took place.

Suddenly, the wife of this relative bent over and started looking for something on the floor. Then she peered under the charpoy. Finally, she went into the adjoining room and started picking and searching through the papers that were lying around.

'What's the matter?' I asked.

With a forced smile and some hesitation, she replied: 'What to say … I had taken out eleven rupees from the knot of my sari and put them on the folding cot. But now they are nowhere to be found …'

'Do you remember it quite clearly that …?'

'Yes, yes, I remember it very well. I had the money tied in my sari knot … I undid the knot to pay the rickshaw puller, then left the cash on the charpoy thinking that I would order four rupees' worth of sweets and give the rest to the kids. We couldn't find a quality sweet shop on the way – we would have brought some with us otherwise. It doesn't look good to visit someone empty-handed. You can realize how embarrassing it is for me now.' Then she leaned towards me and spoke softly: 'Please ask *him*. He came and stood here for some time before going outside swiftly.'

'No, no. He's not that sort,' I told her.

'You do not know these people are experts in this art,' replied the relative in English.

I gave a sidelong cast at Bahadur. With head lowered, he was busy kneading dough. There was a calm and contented look on his face. He had never indulged in such an act. On the contrary, if he ever found a couple of pennies lying around, he put them straight into Nirmala's hands. But how can one know the matters of someone else's heart?

All of a sudden, I did not know what overpowered me – I went into a rage.

'Bahadur!' I called out to him in a stern voice.

'Yes, Babuji?'

'Come here.'

He came and stood in front of me.

'Did you take money from here?'

'No, Babuji!' He answered fearlessly.

'Tell me honestly … I won't be angry.'

'No, Babuji. Had I taken it, I would have told you.'

'Were you not standing here?' said the wife of the relative. 'Then you went out swiftly. Please, speak the truth. I had kept the money to buy sweets and for distributing among the children. Now I am in trouble – there is not even any money left to pay the rickshaw fare back home.'

'But I had gone out to get salt.'

'Speak the truth, Bahadur! If you don't, I will beat you a lot and hand you over to the police,' I shouted.

'I did not take anything, Babuji.' Bahadur's face had turned dark.

I don't know what besieged me. I leapt up abruptly and slapped him across the face. I was expecting that after the slap, he would speak the truth. He barely stopped himself from falling. Tears welled up in his eyes.

'I did not take …'

At this moment the male relative did a strange thing. 'Leave it,' he said, 'we'll take him to the police.' After Saying so, he grabbed Bahadur's hand and dragged him towards the gate. At the door he spoke to him gently: 'Look, if you tell me the truth, I will not do anything but give you a reward of two rupees.'

But Bahadur denied the charge. After that the relative dragged him two or three times towards the gate, as if he were going to take him to the police. But again, he would stop there and start enquiring softly.

Finally, he gave up and left him. He sat on the charpoy and said laughingly, 'Forget it… these people are very thick-skinned and cunning. He may have hidden it in the bushes or buried it deep in the ground. I know them quite well. They are no less than monkeys and bears. Anyway, this much of a loss was predestined.'

After that, Nirmala also threatened Bahadur and slapped him a couple of times. But he kept saying 'no'.

Following this incident, Bahadur was subjected to a lot of beating and scolding. Everyone in the house treated him like a dog. Kishore was almost out for his life. He was now cheerless and unmindful of his duties.

One day I came home late from office. Nirmala was sitting in the courtyard with her head bowed in her hands. None of the boys were home, only the girl was standing beside her mother. The firewood was yet to be lit. The courtyard was dirty; the utensils lay unwashed. The entire house, it seemed, was in a mess.

'What's the matter?' I enquired.

'Bahadur ran away.'

'Ran away!? Why?'

'No idea. Nothing happened today. He was very cheerful since the morning and kept calling me Mataji–Mataji. He had lunch as usual at midday. Afterwards, while he was carrying the *sil-batta* from the courtyard to the veranda, it slipped out of his hands and broke into two. Perhaps he fled thinking that people would beat him for it. But on such a mistake would I have said anything to him? What can I say, perhaps there is no comfort written in my destiny.'

'Did he take anything with him?'

'This is regrettable. He didn't take anything. His clothes, his shoes, his bed – he left behind everything. I have no idea what he thought of us! Would I have stopped him had he asked me before leaving? Rather, I would have sent him off dressed in better clothes, put his salary in his hands. I would even have given him a couple of rupees extra. But he did not take anything ...'

'And those eleven rupees?'

'Ah, that was all lies. I knew beforehand that they didn't intend to give anything to our kids, and that's why they made up this swindle to hide their failings and shame. Don't I know them? At times they lose their money on the way; other times, they mistakenly leave it at home. My heart feels so heavy. Kishore is also very remorseful. He searched the whole town for Bahadur, but to no avail. Kishore returned and said, "Amma, if Bahadur comes back once, I'll hold him tight and not let him to go. I will beg his forgiveness and vow not to beat him again." True! we may never find such a servant again. How much comfort he has bestowed upon us. Had he stolen anything I would, at least, have felt contented.'

Lifting a corner of her sari to her eyes, Nirmala started crying. I was fuming with anger. I wanted to scream but I felt a numbness inside, as if my heart was sinking. I sat on the charpoy with my head down, feeling very low about myself. If I had not beaten him, he would not have left.

I glanced across the courtyard. His bed was folded on the stool in the corner. Some of his clothes were on the rope hanger. Beneath the stool was a pair of brown shoes, which belonged to my brother-in-law's son. I got up and went over to the hanger. I inserted my hand into the pocket of his shorts and started taking out his belongings – the same marble balls, an old deck of playing cards, some beautiful pebbles, pen knives, paper boats …

Dajyu

SHEKHAR JOSHI

A stone's throw from the chowk towards the left was the small cafe with a big signboard where Jagdish Babu had seen him for the first time. Extremely fair-complexioned with bright, blue eyes, gold-tinged hair and a uniquely playful, but not languorous, gait. Agile like a drop of dew dancing on a lotus leaf. The playfulness in his eyes suggested that his age could not be more than nine or ten years, and, most likely, he indeed was of that age. When, after taking a long drag of a half-smoked cigarette, Jagdish Babu entered the cafe, the boy was collecting plates from a table. By the time Jagdish Babu found a chair to settle down, the boy stood right before him, as if he had been waiting for hours for the occupant of that chair. He didn't say anything; he certainly bowed a little and smiled in a gesture of politeness. The entire 'menu', it appeared, flashed through his quiet smile. Receiving the order for a 'single chai', he smiled again and left. A cup of tea appeared before Jagdish Babu within a blink of an eye.

Human emotions are really strange. Despite being alone in a deserted place, one doesn't always feel lonely. One may experience closeness and intimacy even in solitude. Sometimes, on the contrary, one may sense loneliness even amidst the din generated by multitudes. Everything appears totally alien and distant. There is a reason for this. Feelings of loneliness and alienation have their roots in certain narratives of separation and disenchantment.

Jagdish Babu had come from a faraway land, and he felt lonely even in the bustle of the chowk and the hubbub of the cafe. After spending some time and getting used to his environment, he thought he might develop an attachment and intimacy to the place. But as of now he felt the place was indifferent, beyond the limits of exuding any affect and intimacy. And, then, suddenly memories began flooding his mind – memories of people from his village and neighbourhoods of boys from school and college, of cafes and restaurants in his neighbouring town ...

'*Shaab*, chai!'

Jagdish Babu stubbed his cigarette into the ashtray. The sound of these words, he felt, contained exactly the things he was missing here. He began clarifying his hunches.

'What is your name?'

'Madan.'

'Okay! So, Madan, where are you from?'

'I come from the hills, Babuji.'

'There are hundreds of hills – Abu, Darjeeling, Mussoorie, Simla, Almora! In which of these hills is your village?'

Having realized the difference between a hill and a district, he said with a smile, 'Almora, shaab, it's Almora.'

'Which village in Almora?' Jagdish Babu wanted to know more.

This question put Madan in reticence. Perhaps it was the awkward name of his village that embarrassed him. So dodging the question, he replied, 'Shaab, it is quite far from Almora, fifteen–twenty miles away.'

'Okay, but it must have a name,' Jagdish Babu insisted.

'Dotyalagon,' he said hesitatingly.

The coat of solitude painted on Jagdish Babu's face vanished and when he smilingly told Madan that he too came from a nearby village, Madan's almost dropped the tray in excitement. He wanted to say something but couldn't; words froze in his mouth. Looking lost, it appeared, he was trying to go back to his past again and again.

Past – village … high hills … river … Ija … Baba … Didi … Bhuli … Dajyu …!

Whose shadow did Madan see in Jagdish Babu's face? *Ija*? No. *Baba*? No. *Didi … Bhuli*? No. *Dajyu*? Yes, Dajyu!

The chasm of strangeness between Madan and Jagdish Babu disappeared within a couple of days. As soon as Jagdish Babu sat at the table, Madan would salute, 'Dajyu, *jaihinn*.'[1]

'Dajyu, it's very cold today.'

'Dajyu, will it be snowing here too?'

'Dajyu, you ate so little yesterday.' And when came the shout, 'Boy!' Madan would rush to the table before the echo of the call would end. After taking the order from other customers he would walk past Jagdish Babu's table and ask, 'Dajyu, you need anything else?'

'Get a glass of water.'

'Right away, Dajyu.' Madan's voice could be heard from the other side of the cafe.

Madan chanted the word 'dajyu' with the same eagerness and affection as a mother would kiss her long-separated child. Jagdish Babu's loneliness had disappeared in a matter of days. Not only the cafe and the Chowk but the entire city, he felt, was his own, painted in the colour of affect and intimacy. But now he didn't like being called 'dajyu' with such indiscreet frequency. And here was this Madan who would shout from the other table at the far end, 'Dajyu ...!'

'Madan, come here!'

'Coming, Dajyu.'

Repetition of the word 'dajyu' offended Jagdish Babu's middle-class predispositions. The thin thread of affection could not withstand the ferocity of his class pride.

'Dajyu, should I get you a cup of tea?'

'No. And, why do you keep chanting 'dajyu-dajyu' all the time? Don't you care for anyone's *prestige*?'

Jagdish Babu's face turned red with anger, he couldn't control his words. Whether Madan would understand the meaning of prestige or not, he didn't even notice. But Madan certainly understood, without any explanation.

Madan was deeply hurt with Jagdish Babu's behaviour. Citing the excuse of a headache to the manager, he slipped inside a room and, putting his head between his knees, cried inconsolably. Far away from his home and country that he was, it was quite natural for Madan to display his affection for Jagdish Babu. That is the reason why today for the first time in his migrant life he felt as if someone had forcibly dragged him down from his mother's lap, father's embrace and sister's soothing shade.

However, sentimentality is transient. Letting all the inner pain roll out in the form of tears, one feels cleansed and unburdened, and whatever course of action one then decides on is often more rational than a decision taken during turbulent moments.

Madan began working as before.

The next day, Jagdish Babu ran into his childhood classmate Hemant. After entering the cafe, Jagdish Babu gestured Madan to come over to his table. He felt that Madan was trying to avoid him. The boy arrived at the table only on his second call. Not only was his usual smile missing, he also did not say what he used to, 'Dajyu, what should I get for you?' It was left for Jagdish Babu to spell out, 'Two teas, two omelettes.' Instead of replying, 'Right away, Dajyu,' Madan said, 'Right away, Shaab.' As if they were strangers.

'Seems to be from the hills?' Hemant speculated.

'Yes,' replied Jagdish Babu disinterestedly and changed the track of conversation.

Madan had arrived with the tea.

'What is your name, boy?' Hemant asked in a patronizing tone.

For a few moments, there was a stony silence at the table. Jagdish Babu kept staring at his cup. Past memories swirled before Madan's eyes – Jagdish Babu asking his name one day … then … 'Dajyu you ate so little yesterday'… and finally, 'Don't you care for anyone's *prestige*?'

Jagdish Babu raised his eyes and looked at him and felt that Madan might erupt like a volcano.

Hemant repeated the question in an imploring voice, 'What is your name?'

'Shaab, I am called *boy*.' Madan left after this curt reply. His rage-fuelled face had turned red and looked even more beautiful.

Notes on the Stories

Introduction

1. 'Child Domestic Labour-A Modern Form of Feudalism', Global March, 11 June 2013. Available: https://globalmarch.org/child-domestic-labour-a-modern-form-of-feudalism/
2. A helpful summary of these efforts can be found in Jeet Singh, 'Domestic Workers and Policy Discourse in India', 21 September 2017. Available: https://www.rgics.org/wp-content/uploads/policy-issue-briefs/Issue-Brief-Domestic-Workers-and-Policies-September-2017.pdf
3. Since we undertook this project of translation in mid-2017, Premchand's stories have been translated in 2018 by M. Asaduddin.

3. He Was a Thief

1. A servant category that first became 'bearer' in the Anglicized dictum of the eighteenth and nineteenth centuries.

4. Mangar

1. The references are to Jørgen Peter Müller and Eugen Sandow. Müller and Sandow were the leading lights of the Physical Culture Movement in early twentieth-century Europe.

Müller's book *My System* (1904) discusses his philosophy of health and provides photographic guidelines for natural exercises. His ideal of perfect physique, however, was different from Sandow's. Sandow was also one of the earliest professional bodybuilders, a proponent of gym exercise and a showman. Both of them were well known among the early twentieth-century Indian youth. In the late 1920s and 1930s, Indian cities and towns also witnessed a wave of the Physical Culture Movement; Yuvak Sanghas (youth leagues) were established in almost all Indian cities. Rambriksha Benipuri, the author of this story, was a member of Patna Yuvak Sangha; he also edited a journal *Yuvak* (1929), which was banned within a couple of years due to charges of seditious publication.

5. Rama

1. This is a saying in Hindi, '*bandar naach dikhaane aaya*'.
2. The expression in Hindi '*roothi ladki kaun manave, garaj padi to daudi aawe*', is a popular saying.

6. Sabia

1. It is important to note that some of the authors chose to depict the poverty-stricken bodily appearance of these children as nothing more than a lump of flesh.

7. Ratnaprabha

1. *Chhabili Bhatiyari* and *Tota-Maina* were considered to be erotic/obscene literature. At pilgrimage centres and markets, the peddlers often sold such erotic literature and other sex manuals like *Kokshashtra* alongside religious tracts and moral treatises like *Hanuman-Chalisa* and *Stri-Subodhini*.

2. It should be noticeable to the readers that in the climax, the young boy who is bound to Ratnaprabha in service, doing *naukri* and *bandagi*, addresses her with the non-respect pronoun of you (*tum*).

11. Dajyu

1. This is a spoken form of the salutation 'Jai Hind' (Victory to India), which was first used by the Indian National Army. After Independence, it was adopted by the Indian Army, and nowadays it is widely used in the institutions of police and bureaucracy. Due to a long tradition of conscription in hilly areas, perhaps the same expression became a general form of greeting.

Notes on the Authors

Premchand (1880–1936), possibly the best-known Hindi-Urdu author of the last two centuries, was born in Lamhi, a village in Uttar Pradesh's Banaras district. He had begun writing in Urdu from 1907. After his first collection *Soz-e-Vatan* (1909) was proscribed, he changed his pen name from Nawab Rai to Premchand. He switched over to writing in Hindi around 1913–15. He started his own printing press; he edited and published *Jagaran* and *Hans*. The latter became one of the leading magazines of the Hindi literary world. At Gandhi's call, along with Jainendra Kumar, he actively supported the cause of Hindustani against (anti-Muslim) proponents of exclusivist Hindi. In this period, he also drew closer to the leftist intellectual writers' collective and presided over the first conference of the Progressive Writers' Association in Lucknow in 1936. His multi-volume collection of short stories, *Mansarovar*, and his novels *Sevasadan*, *Premashram*, *Rangbhumi*, *Karmabhumi* and *Godan* are considered modern Indian classics.

Mahadevi Varma (1902–87) was one of the earliest woman poets, writers and educationists known for her distinctive literary sensibility and public life among the men of Hindi letters. Under Gandhi's influence, she took to wearing khadi and teaching in two village schools outside Allahabad during the 1930s. She became the principal of the nationalist educational institution, Mahila Vidyapeeth College. She was soon recognized as a major poet of the *Chhayavadi* or romantic school of Hindi poetry along with Suryakant Tripathi 'Nirala', Jaishankar Prasad and Sumitranandan Pant. Her limited but outstanding ornate prose in the collection of character sketches *Atit ke Chalchitra*, from which we have translated two stories included in this volume, and *Shrinkhala ki Kadiyan* are recognized for their stylistic uniqueness in Hindi literature. She was also the recipient of many awards including the Sahitya Akademi, Jnanpith and Padma Vibhushan.

Rambriksha Benipuri (1899–1968) was a writer, journalist and politician born in the small village of Benipur in the Muzaffarpur district of Bihar. Known for his flowery language and sentimentalism, his literary oeuvre includes not only stories, sketches and personal essays but historical plays, novels, memoirs, travelogues, biographies and children's stories. Benipuri emerged as one of the prominent socialist leaders in Bihar and was also elected as an Member of Legislative Assembly (MLA) in the 1957 state election. He later (re-)published a major part of his scattered sketches, stories, and novels in the first volume of his collected works, *Benipuri Granthavali*. The two stories translated in this collection are from the first volume. The rest of the volumes could not be published during his lifetime.

Jainendra Kumar (1905–88) was born as Anandi Lal in Kaudiyaganj village in Uttar Pradesh's Aligarh district. His pioneering literary works are acclaimed for developing a new sensibility and subjectivity in Hindi literature. His novels and stories explore the psycho-sexual self and interiority of his characters, especially young and educated women, with bare social and exterior details. His first collection of stories, *Phansi*, was published in 1930. His first novel *Parakh* (1929) was awarded the Hindustani Academy Prize in 1931. He also edited many political and literary journals. He grew very close to Premchand. After the latter's death, Kumar became the editor of *Hans*. On Gandhi's call, along with Premchand, he was actively involved in the founding of the Hindustani Sabha that decried the anti-Urdu position of Hindi chauvinism. Apart from many novels and innumerable stories, he also wrote on issues pertaining to literature, culture and aesthetics. He was the recipient of many awards, including the Sahitya Akademi and Padma Bhushan.

Saadat Hasan Manto (1912–55), one of the best-known Urdu short-story writers of the last century, was born in Samrala near Ludhiana in Punjab. His foray into literature began as an Urdu translator of English, French and Russian classics in the early 1930s. Soon, he established himself as short-story writer par excellence. He also worked at All India Radio as well as the Bombay film industry and remained closely associated with the latter until the Partition. He left Bombay for Pakistan and in the last years of his extremely short life, he became an alcoholic and died of liver cirrhosis in Lahore. He wrote more than twenty collections of short stories, a novel and many radio plays. *Aatish Paray*, *Teen Auraten* and *Siah Hasiye* are his most well-known collections. Many of his stories distinctively deal with gruesome and traumatic experiences of the Partition, especially the horrors of physical and sexual violence.

Upendra Nath 'Ashk' (1910–96) was a novelist, short-story writer and playwright. He was born in Jalandhar, Punjab. After finishing his graduation in Lahore, he worked as a reporter in Lala Lajpat Rai's daily, *Vande Mataram*. 'Ashk' began his literary career in Urdu but switched over to Hindi on the advice of Premchand in 1933. He also worked for All India Radio in the early 1940s and later went to Bombay to work with *Filmistan*, a noted film production house of the time. In Bombay, he also developed a close association with Indian People's Theatre Association (IPTA). After almost a decade-long stint in Bombay films, he settled in Allahabad and successfully ran a publication house named Neelabh Prakashan. *Girti Diwaren* and its six sequels are his critically acclaimed novels. Apart from his collections of seventy short stories and twenty-five one-act plays, his two memoirs on contemporary litterateurs are also well known. He was also a playwright par excellence and the first Hindi dramatist to receive the Sangeet Natak Akademi Award.

Amarkant (1925–2014) was a Hindi short-story writer and novelist. Born in Nagara village of Uttar Pradesh's Ballia district, he graduated from Allahabad University. A socialist in his political orientation, he had participated in the Quit India Movement of 1942 against the then British government. Later, he wrote a novel on the same historical event, *Inhi Hathiyaron Se*, for which he received the Sahitya Akademi Award. Initially, he worked as a journalist, but later established himself as a leading storyteller who, in piquantly simple prose, narrated the problems and pathos of everyday lives in small towns of north India. He wrote more than a dozen novels and published many collections of short stories. He also wrote excellent stories for children as well as autobiographical memoirs. *Jindagi aur Jonk*, *Dopahar ka Bhojan*, *Dipti-Kalektri* (short stories), and *Sunnar Pande ki Patohu* (novel) are some of his most famous works. He was also honoured with the prestigious Jnanpith Award.

Shekhar Joshi (b. 1932) belongs to Almora district, Uttarakhand. He received his early education in Dehradun. At a very young age, he marked his literary debut in 1956 with the short story 'Dajyu', which was later made into a children's film by the Children's Film Society of India. Critically acclaimed for his economy of language and simplicity of prose, his literary oeuvre deals largely with the 'lesser' lives in the hills, modern industrial factories, and little-explored predicaments of the urban middle classes. 'Koshi ka Ghatwar', 'Aakhiri Tukda' and 'Badboo' are his other well-known stories. He currently lives in Allahabad.

Glossary

Aghan	the months of November–December
Amlah	the revenue collectors of zamindars
Ashwamedha	a royal ritual in which a horse is sacrificed
Aurat jaat	woman (literally 'of the caste of women', a derogatory, patriarchal reference)
Bachiya	young girl
Badi-papad	dried lentil balls and poppadum
Bandagi	in service or servitude
Bawarchi	chef
Bera	waiter/bearer
Bhaat	cooked rice
Bhang	edible cannabis
Bhangi	a caste group of toilet-cleaners and sweepers
Bhuli	younger sister
Bibi/Bibiji	mistress
Chakravyuh	a circular battle formation deceptive to the enemy as once a person is inside, the exit routes close from behind
Charkha	a spinning wheel
Chaitra	the months of March–April
Chaubara	a house with four doors/a concubine's house
Chowk	square

Daal-chawal	cooked lentils and rice
Dafli	tambourine
Dajyu	elder brother
Darshan	praying and seeing any god's idol
Datun	twig/chew stick
Deviji	lady/wife
Fez	Rumi cap
Ganja	marijuana
Gaz	unit of length
Gondani	*Cordia gharaf*
Hamel	a necklace made of silver coins
Hantar	whip
Huzoor	sir/madam
Ija	mother
Iron guz	measuring rod
Jaan	beloved
Jaap	chanting god's name
Jamadar	sweeper
Kachahri	zamindar's court
Kaharin	water bearers/maids who considered themselves ritually purer than those who only washed dishes
Kakraunda	*Carissa carandas*
Kaliyug	age symbolized with deprivation and immorality
Kanyadan	the ritual of gifting a daughter in marriage
Khatta	*Citrus limonum*
Lattha	coarse cotton fabric
Lehanga	ankle-length skirt
Maharajin	female cook (usually Brahmin)
Manjhle	middle or number two of three
Mehtarani	sweeper-women

Mirjai	sleeveless jacket
Naukar-chakar	servants
Nazrana	feudal offerings
Pania	water bearer
Pardesh	faraway land
Phagun	the months of January–February
Punya	religious merit
Raisaheb	a colonial rank/honorific bestowed upon loyal zamindars
Raisahebi	vanity of those belonging to the Rai Saheb rank
Ramnami dupatta	a scarf on which Lord Rama's name is printed
Rasoiya	cook
Safa	turban
Sahib	officer/sir
Sala saheb	wife's brother
Sarkar	master/lord
Sasural	in-laws' place
Ser	traditional unit of mass/volume/weight
Seth	merchant-banker
Sethani	merchant-banker's wife
Shaab	sir/boss/master
Shamiyana	canopy
Sil-batta	stone spice grinder
sudarashan chakra	circular weapon of Lord Vishnu
Thakurji	idol
Thanedar	police inspector
Vaitarni	name of a dangerous river to be crossed before entering the gates of heaven
Virasan, yogasan	names of yoga positions

Acknowledgements

This book was conceived by us in the course of the first international conference entitled Servants' Pasts held at the Centre for Studies of Developing Societies (CSDS), New Delhi, in February 2017. The conference was part of the research project 'Domestic Servants in Colonial South Asia', funded by the European Research Council (ERC-Stg 640627, 2015–18). We would like to thank the ERC for funding this project, without which such a volume for a wider readership would not have become possible. We would like to thank Sri Karmendu Shishir, Rajeev Ranjan Giri, Rakesh Pandey, Ramayan Ram, Ravikant and Uday Shankar for helping us in the curation and selection of stories. Our special thanks to Sri Shekhar Joshi ji for communicating his kind approval and encouragement through his son Sanjay Joshi. We wish him a long and healthy life. Many thanks are also due to Sri Arvind Kumar ji, son of Sri Amarkant, for his encouragement and support. We would also like to thank Deepmala Gupta for preparing, on demand, a representative pencil sketch which makes visible the presence of the servant working in the household and beyond. We are grateful to the known and unknown online handler–contributors of Hindisamay.com, Gadyakosh.org, Rekhta, Archive.org and YouTube for making the Hindi–Urdu literary world easily accessible and audible for everyone. Finally, our sincere and heartfelt thanks go to Prasun Chatterjee at Pan Macmillan India whose intervention was crucial in turning a faint idea into a published book.

Nitin Sinha
ZMO, Berlin

Prabhat Kumar
CSDS, Delhi